Filmmaker SHANE BLACK on the Work of BRETT HALLIDAY

"In this age of private eyes with cats, funny neighbors, and relationship woes—here's to 40's thriller writer Brett Halliday, whose baffling, bullet-paced capers have come to light again.

"Halliday's books were marvels of misdirection. Red herrings, skewed motives, mistaken identities—he did everything but come to your house and bang cymbals.

"Halliday's plots are byzantine gems. This is back when mystery writers were so much *smarter* than you and me. Want an engrossing read? Pick this one up.

"Never heard of this book? No matter. It's been waiting patiently, poised to dazzle you with raw, ingenious storytelling. Halliday is the king of the baffler novel. Pure pleasure.

"How long can Halliday's best-selling books remain dormant, undiscovered…? The answer: not a minute longer, thanks to Hard Case Crime."

Shane Black is the author of numerous films including LETHAL WEAPON, THE LONG KISS GOODNIGHT, and KISS KISS BANG BANG, which was partly inspired by the books of Brett Halliday.

The door of his hotel room stood slightly ajar when he returned. He know he had locked it when he went out.

He went on around the corner of the corridor and stopped. He took his time about lighting a cigarette, moving back to a position where he could watch the door.

The incident didn't make much sense to Shayne. If this was an ambush, the person inside his room was playing it dumb to leave the door open to warn him. On the other hand, he realized fully that he had stayed alive for a lot of precarious years by never taking anything for granted.

He smoked his cigarette down to a short butt, then walked rapidly along the corridor, drawing his gun as he approached his door from the wrong direction.

He hit the open door with his left shoulder in a lunge that carried him well into the center of the room.

A woman sat in a chair by the window. She dropped a water tumbler from which she had been helping herself to his cognac. Otherwise she remained perfectly calm.

Shayne's alert gray eyes swiftly circled the room, returning to her face while he slowly pocketed the gun.

"Carmela Towne," he said in a flat tone.

Carmela pushed herself up from the chair with both hands gripping the arms. Her eyes searched his face and she said, "Michael," making three syllables of his name, her voice throaty and a little blurred.

"Some day you'll get yourself shot," he said, and went toward her.

Carmela Towne giggled, "I'm already half-shot, Michael," and held out her arms to him...

MURDER *is* *my* BUSINESS

by Brett Halliday

A HARD CASE CRIME NOVEL

A HARD CASE CRIME BOOK

(HCC-066)

August 2010

Published by

Dorchester Publishing Co., Inc.
200 Madison Avenue
New York, NY 10016

in collaboration with Winterfall LLC

This book is a work of fiction. Names, characters, places, and incidents either are the products of the author's imagination or are used fictitiously, and any resemblance to actual events or persons, living or dead, is entirely coincidental.

ISBN 0-8439-6328-X
ISBN-13 978-0-8439-6328-1

Cover design by Cooley Design Lab

Typeset by Swordsmith Productions

The name "Hard Case Crime" and the Hard Case Crime logo are trademarks of Winterfall LLC. Hard Case Crime books are selected and edited by Charles Ardai.

Printed in the United States of America

Visit us on the web at www.HardCaseCrime.com

For FORREST and HELEN FISHEL
In appreciation of so many things.

CHAPTER ONE

On a late fall day in 1944 Michael Shayne was slouched in his swivel chair half asleep when his secretary quietly opened the door to his private office and stepped inside. A felt hat was tipped forward, the brim shading his eyes, and his big feet rested comfortably on his scarred oak desk.

Lucy Hamilton closed the door firmly and advanced toward him. Shayne roused, cocked a shaggy red eyebrow upward, and muttered, "Go away."

Lucy was slim and straight and supple. She had clear brown eyes and a sweetly rounded face with a firm chin. She said, "No wonder you don't get ahead in this competitive world. There's a client outside."

Shayne yawned and stretched his long arms, then opened both eyes. "I was dreaming," he said accusingly. "A damned nice dream. And then I saw you standing there. Is the door locked?" He swung his feet down purposefully and started to get up.

Lucy backed away from him. She said, "I never lock the door when I come in here," with crisp dignity. "Shall I send the lady in?"

Shayne scowled and sank back into the creaking swivel chair. "Is she pretty?"

"No. She's a little old lady."

"Money?"

"I'm afraid not. But she's terribly worried about her boy."

Shayne said, "Nuts." His scowl deepened. He pulled off his limp felt hat and sailed it across the room, where it landed on top of a steel filing cabinet. He ran knobby fingers through his bristly red hair and growled, "Why do I always have to draw old ladies without any money? If you were the right kind of secretary—"

Lucy Hamilton had her hand on the doorknob. She opened the door and said, "Mr. Shayne will be pleased to see you, Mrs. Delray." She stood aside to let the little old lady enter the office.

Mrs. Delray was shrunken and brisk. She wore a voluminous black silk dress that reached almost to her ankles, and an outmoded black hat flared up and away from her wrinkled face. She had a sweet smile and an air of quiet dignity that brought Shayne up from his chair. He said, "I'm sorry my secretary kept you waiting, Mrs. Delray. If you'll take this chair—"

Mrs. Delray perched herself on the edge of a wooden chair beside Shayne's desk. The tips of her black, substantial shoes barely touched the floor. "Captain Denton recommended you, Mr. Shayne," she began at once. "He said I should see a private detective and you were the cheapest one in New Orleans. You see, I haven't very much money to spend." She spoke briskly, leaning toward him, her black eyes bright and expectant.

Shayne slid into his chair and folded his arms on the desk. He said, "Captain Denton, eh?" without enthusiasm. "Is he a friend of yours, Mrs. Delray?"

"Oh—no. I don't know any policemen. I went to his

office for help, but it seems that policemen aren't interested in helping a taxpayer. He said I'd have to hire a private detective and he hustled me right out of his office."

"Why do you need a detective?" he asked with gentle restraint.

"It's about my boy, Jimmie. He's a good boy and he's not a draft-dodger, Mr. Shayne." Her voice trembled with eagerness to be believed. She fumbled with the clasp of a large, worn pocketbook and drew out an envelope. She offered it to Shayne, explaining, "This is a letter I got from Jimmie this morning. You can see he's as patriotic as anybody even if he didn't ever register for the draft like it seems he should have."

Shayne took the envelope and pulled out two folded sheets of USO writing paper covered on both sides with penciled words. He settled back and read:

Dear Ma—

Here I am back in the U.S.A. after five years. A lot of things have happened since I wrote to you a couple of months ago. I haven't got time to tell you all of them, but it looks like I am going to get a chance to make up for staying out of the War all this time while I was working in Mexico.

Like I told you before, I didn't know I was supposed to register for the draft while I was in Mexico, and when I found out about the law last year I was afraid to on account of I thought they might arrest me for a draft-dodger.

But I felt guilty about it and finally couldn't stand

it any longer and came back to El Paso. And then a funny thing happened, Ma. It's like in a storybook. I met up with a man and got to talking to him and he said why didn't I go to the Army and tell them the truth about being in Mexico all this time and ask to enlist, only not under my real name on account of it might cause trouble for you and because there's big things happening here and they need me for sort of undercover snooping because I can talk Mexican good and ain't enlisted under my real name and all that.

I can't tell you any more about it, Ma, because I don't know much more, but it's some sort of spy ring and it's awful exciting and maybe I'll be a hero after all.

So when you write to me address your letters to Private James Brown at the above address and don't worry about it being anything wrong on account of I think you'll be proud of me when it's all over.

I've got a pass to go into town this afternoon and meet this man and find out more about it.

I will close in haste.

Your loving son, Jim.

Mrs. Delray watched him eagerly. She said, "You can see for yourself, Mr. Shayne, Jimmie's wanting to do the right thing."

He muttered, "Yeah," absently. His right thumb and forefinger gently massaged his left earlobe as he frowned at Jim Delray's letter, his gray eyes brooding upon the penciled sheets.

Carefully refolding it and replacing it in the envelope, he looked up to meet the mother's bright eyes. He shrugged his wide shoulders and said, "I don't see why you need a detective, Mrs. Delray. If you want to take this up with anyone, I suggest you go to the FBI."

Fear clouded her lined face. "I'm afraid to," she confessed. "I don't know what they might do to Jimmie when they find out he was working in Mexico for five years and didn't ever even register for the draft like the law says. And now he's gone and enlisted under a false name and all—" Her voice trembled and there were tears in her eyes, but she lifted her chin proudly. "Not that my Jimmie would do anything wrong, Mr. Shayne. He's a good boy and he's been *that* worried about not getting registered."

"What sort of work was he doing in Mexico?" Shayne asked idly.

"Driving a truck for a mine, the *Plata Azul* mine, they call it. But he really didn't know about the draft until last year."

Shayne lit a cigarette and suggested, "Why not let things go along as they are? If your son has actually got on to some sort of spy ring in El Paso and if he succeeds in exposing them, I'm certain the government will forgive him for enlisting under a false name."

"But that isn't all of it," she said hastily, fumbling in her purse again. She brought out a clipping torn from a local newspaper and passed it to Shayne.

"Right after getting Jimmie's letter this morning I happened to see this in the paper. It's—well—you can read it for yourself." There was a queer urgency in her old voice, a sort of harsh vibrancy that was at the same time proud and pleading.

It was an AP dispatch, datelined the preceding day from El Paso, Texas. It stated that Private James Brown, a recent recruit at Fort Bliss, had died that afternoon in an auto-pedestrian accident, receiving injuries that were instantly fatal underneath the wheels of a limousine owned and driven by Mr. Jefferson Towne, local smelter magnate and candidate for the mayoralty of El Paso on a Citizen's Reform ticket.

Details of the accident were vague in the brief account, but it was assumed that the soldier had stumbled or fallen into the path of the oncoming limousine; and Mr. Towne's humanity and citizenship were lauded due to the fact that though there were no witnesses, the candidate stopped immediately and rendered what assistance he could and then made a prompt and full report to the authorities despite the fact that such action might prove detrimental to his political aspirations.

Chief of Police C. E. Dyer stated that Mr. Towne had been released on his own recognizance and expressed the personal belief that the accident had been unavoidable, though he promised the citizens of El Paso a full investigation. The dispatch also stated that the parents of Private James Brown in Cleveland, Ohio, were being notified of their son's death by army authorities.

Three vertical lines in Shayne's forehead deepened into trenches as he read the dispatch with great care. He looked up to ask, "When was your son's letter written, Mrs. Delray?"

"Yesterday morning. He sent it airmail. And he said

he had a pass to go to town and see some man about the spy business in the afternoon. Do you suppose—it *wasn't* an accident, Mr. Shayne?"

Shayne shook his head. "I happen to know Jeff Towne. Knew him ten years ago," he amended, "and I'm certain Towne isn't the type to be mixed up in a spy ring." He glanced down at the dispatch and muttered, "Running for mayor? He must have been doing all right these past ten years."

"But there must be some reason for it." Mrs. Delray's voice trembled urgently. "Couldn't be just happenstance."

"You're not certain the James Brown mentioned here is your son," Shayne reminded her. "It's a very common name. And this James Brown appears to have parents in Cleveland, Ohio."

"It's my Jimmie. I know it is. He wouldn't tell the truth about where his folks live, I guess, enlisting under a different name and all."

Shayne nodded, his gaunt face hardening a little. He looked past the bonneted mother, out through open windows of his fourth-floor office in the International Building to the soft blue of the horizon. His eyes narrowed a little and a muscle jumped in the left side of his lean jaw. He said, "I'll check with El Paso, Mrs. Delray. If they haven't succeeded in locating the dead soldier's parents in Cleveland, I'll take the case."

"Will you, Mr. Shayne? Like I said at first, I haven't got much money to spend—"

Shayne's outflung hand silenced her. "Didn't Captain Denton tell you I could be had cheaply?" He lifted his voice to call, Lucy. She appeared in the doorway almost immediately.

"Get Chief of Police Dyer in El Paso, Texas, on the phone," Shayne directed her. "If you can't reach Dyer, try to get Captain Gerlach." Lucy nodded and went back into the reception room.

"I know it's my Jimmie," Mrs. Delray said again with complete conviction. "I just sort of feel it like, Mr. Shayne. And it's got something to do with those spies that talked him into enlisting under a false name. Jimmie wasn't any coward and they must have seen he wouldn't help them out."

Shayne nodded absently. He got up and walked across to the double windows. It was warm and quiet in the office. Through the open door into the reception room came the murmur of Lucy Hamilton's voice as she put through his long-distance call.

Shayne thrust both big hands deep into his pockets and scowled savagely out at New Orleans' skyline. He had one of those crazy hunches that hit him like a ton of bricks sometimes. It was a feeling he couldn't put his finger on, but one that he had long ago learned could not be disregarded. He stiffened and wheeled about when his secretary called, "I have Chief Dyer on the line, Mr. Shayne."

He strode past Mrs. Delray to pick up a telephone on his desk. "Hello. Dyer? Mike Shayne speaking. That's right, it has been a hell of a long time. I'm checking on the traffic death of a soldier in El Paso yesterday. Private James Brown. Has the army been able to locate his parents in Cleveland?"

Shayne listened intently, and as he listened the deep lines in his forehead gradually smoothed out. He nodded after a time and his voice was almost exuberant when he agreed: "It does look as though the James Brown and Cleveland address might be a phony, doesn't it? I'll be up tomorrow and may have some dope on that, but keep it under your hat. In the meantime, do me a favor, Chief, and yourself one too. Pull an autopsy on the corpse. What? I don't care if the cause of death *is* established. Yep. Be seeing you."

Shayne replaced the telephone on its prongs and told Mrs. Delray, "I'm afraid it may be your son. The Cleveland address simply doesn't exist, and they have no record of him there."

"I knew it." Mrs. Delray clenched her thin hands together convulsively. "But I don't know whether I can afford to pay your expenses to make a trip up there, Mr. Shayne. I've got fifty dollars here—"

She was nervously opening her purse again, but Shayne stopped her with a wave of his big hand. "The spy angle makes this sort of government business, Mrs. Delray. Forget about the expenses. They'll be taken care of."

Tears of thankfulness came into her old eyes. "That's what I asked Captain Denton—if the government wouldn't do something. He just laughed and said they couldn't follow up every wild-goose chase that came along. But will you have to tell them, Mr. Shayne, about Jimmie?"

Shayne shook his head. "I won't have to tell anyone anything." He patted her shoulder gently. "You go on home and try not to worry. I'll get in touch with you as soon as I have something to report. Just leave your address with my secretary." He helped her from the chair and toward the door.

Lucy came in a few minutes later and stopped in front of his desk with her hands belligerently on her hips. "You certainly let Captain Denton put a sweet one over on you this time. Just forget about the expenses, Mrs. Delray. Where are we going to get next month's office rent?"

Shayne grinned and opened a drawer to get out a bottle of cognac and two four-ounce glasses. "We've still got a drink left. Relax and have one with me."

"As long as you've got a drink of cognac, you don't think about expenses," she charged, her brown eyes blazing with wrath.

Shayne's grin widened. He poured one glass full and looked at her inquiringly. She shook her head and took a backward step. "You just want to get me woozy so I won't mind if you go off on a trip to El Paso."

He lifted his glass and arched his eyebrows at her. "Why, Lucy. I didn't realize you *would* mind."

"I don't. Not the way you think. I hate to see you fall for a sob story like that. No wonder Captain Denton told her you could be had cheaply."

Shayne tossed off the cognac and laughed. "Get me a reservation on the next plane for El Paso. If I need a priority, get in touch with Captain Campbell, Military Intelligence." He gave her a telephone number.

Lucy's brown eyes widened. "Do you really think it's a spy ring?"

"I doubt it, but there should be enough in the story to wangle me a priority for plane space."

The sparkle went out of Lucy's eyes. "Just another one of your shenanigans. What am I going to tell Mr. Pontiff Jalreaux when he calls tomorrow?"

"Tell him any damned thing you want to," Shayne told her impatiently.

"That you're in El Paso on a charity case?"

Shayne poured his glass half full of cognac again. "There'll be certain compensations for my trip to El Paso," he assured her gravely. "You see, I knew Jeff Towne ten years ago. I did a little job for him while I was working with World-Wide. He had a daughter. She was twenty. Her mother was Spanish." He emptied his glass and smacked his lips. "Carmela will be thirty now. A beautiful and frustrated thirty." He set his glass down and there was a queer gleam in his eyes.

"She'll be fat and satisfied," Lucy warned him. "All Spanish women are at thirty."

"Not Carmela Towne. She won't be married—unless Towne has changed a lot. That's the job I did for him. There was a chap named Lance Bayliss. A poet, Lucy, and a poet is lower than dirt to a two-fisted, self-made financier like Jefferson Towne. He broke up their engagement and he broke Carmela's heart. I doubt whether she's looked at another man."

"So you expect her to welcome you with open arms?"

Shayne grinned crookedly. "I'd like to see what the years have done to Carmela Towne," he assented. "And to her father. He was on his way up ten years ago, rough and ruthless and domineering. Now he seems to be at the top of the heap, local magnate and mayoralty candidate." He scowled at his glass. "He must have changed a great deal since I knew him—though I didn't think Jeff Towne could ever change."

"What made you ask for an autopsy on the soldier?" Lucy asked him. "I read the letter and the clipping before you saw Mrs. Delray, and I don't see why you think it wasn't just a traffic accident."

Shayne looked at her in surprise. "I've just been telling you."

"You've been mooning about a half-blooded Spanish girl whom you hope to find frustrated and beautiful," she reminded him bitterly.

Shayne shook his head and complained, "Sometimes I fear you'll never make a detective, Lucy. Call the airport and see about the plane."

CHAPTER TWO

The plane set Michael Shayne down at the El Paso municipal airport early the next morning, and a taxi took him to the old yet still magnificent Paso Del Norte Hotel, where he had reserved a room by wire the preceding evening. He went up for a shave and a quick shower, and then down to the coffee shop for breakfast, picking up a copy of the evening *Free Press* as he went by the newsstand.

He settled himself at a table in a corner of the un-crowded coffee shop and spread the paper out before him. A glance at the front page left no reader in any doubt as to whom the *Free Press* was championing in the mayoralty election. A black headline proclaimed: *Towne Released to Kill Again.*

Shayne ordered coffee and scrambled eggs and settled back to read the story. Stripped of innuendo and inflammatory accusations, it told how Jefferson Towne at dusk the preceding evening had run down and killed a young recruit from nearby Fort Bliss who had been identified as James Brown of Cleveland, Ohio. The opposition paper made much of the fact that Towne had been released by Chief Dyer on his own recognizance to (as the *Free Press* stated it) *go forth and kill again*, and it broadly hinted that the entire police department had joined in a conspiracy to cover up Towne's crime.

The news story concluded with a brief paragraph that caused a slow grin to spread over Shayne's rugged face:

The citizens of El Paso are warned that no effort or expense will be spared by Jefferson Towne to white-wash his criminal negligence in this matter. As we go to press, the Free Press *learns from a reliable source that a private detective of unsavory reputa-tion from New Orleans has been retained to aid in confusing the electorate on this issue and to hide the full truth from our citizens.*

For an interesting commentary on this desperate expedient of Candidate Towne, be sure to read the editorial by our Crime Reporter, Neil Cochrane, on this page.

A waitress brought Shayne's coffee and eggs. He took a sip of coffee and scowled across the room. He remembered Neil Cochrane from ten years ago. Neil had been a friend of Lance Bayliss—and of Carmela Towne. A thin, waspish, eager lad, with a head too big for his undersized body, and a sharp, incisive intellect. Shayne had an idea that Neil, too, had fancied himself in love with Carmela in those days, though he must have known there could be no one but Lance in her life. Now Neil Cochrane was a reporter on the *Free Press*, violently opposing the election of Carmela's father.

Shayne folded the paper and read a boxed editorial near the center of the page. It was starkly titled, *WARNING!*

Jeff Towne is a two-fisted fighting man. Those of us in El Paso who have followed his career with interest during the past decade know this to be true. He is a man accustomed to ride roughshod over his enemies, crushing and casting aside those who oppose him, surging upward through sheer aggressiveness to a position of industrial and financial leadership in this community.

Now, looking for more worlds to conquer, Jeff Towne has acquired political ambitions, and he brings to the political arena those same ruthless characteristics that have not failed him in the past. Jeff Towne is determined to be the next mayor of El Paso!

Yesterday a young soldier died beneath the wheels of Jeff Towne's speeding limousine in the streets of this city. Crushed, as other men have been crushed when they stood in Jeff Towne's way.

Fearful of a public reaction which will smash his political aspirations beneath a landslide of votes for Honest John Carter, Jeff Towne is fighting back!

With a vast fortune at his disposal, Towne has retained the services of a notorious private detective to fly here from New Orleans in a desperate attempt to cover up the true facts in this case.

Some of us in El Paso know Michael Shayne personally, and most of us know of him through newspaper accounts of his past exploits in cleverly circumventing the Law and disproving the guilt of wealthy clients.

The citizens of El Paso are solemnly warned *to*

expect subtle trickery and distortion of facts by this detective when he takes over the case against Jeff Towne. An indication of his methods is his telephonic demand of yesterday upon Chief Dyer that an autopsy be immediately performed upon the body of Towne's victim for the ostensible purpose of ascertaining the cause of death.

An autopsy on a traffic victim!

Yet we learn from Chief Dyer himself that he has weakly acceded to this ridiculous demand and that an autopsy has been ordered.

We await the result of this farcical proceeding with indignation and with interest, and we warn our readers to accept with a grain of salt any medical testimony which attempts to shift the blame for the death of Private James Brown from the shoulders of Candidate Towne where it belongs.

The boxed editorial was signed by Neil Cochrane.

Shayne drank his cup of coffee and ate his scrambled eggs. He got a second cup of coffee and leisurely smoked a cigarette while he drank it. It was 9:30 when he left the hotel and strolled down the street to police headquarters.

Chief Dyer looked up from his desk with a tired smile when a sergeant ushered Shayne into his private office. He shoved aside some papers and leaned forward to shake Shayne's hand heartily, saying, "You didn't waste any time getting here."

"I flew in." Shayne pulled up a chair and sat down.

Chief Dyer was bald, and a complete absence of

cyebrows gave his face a naked look. He had a sharp
nose with vertical creases on each side leading down to
the corners of his mouth. His chin was pointed and
jutted forward aggressively. He smoked cigarettes in a
long holder, and had a way of never looking at a man
when he talked to him. "I don't get this," he complained. "When you telephoned yesterday I assumed
you were acting for Towne, but after the *Free Press*
appeared last night Towne came storming in and swore
he hadn't retained you."

Shayne said, "I just finished reading the *Free Press*."

"Towne's plenty sore," Dyer told him. "He figures it
won't do him a damned bit of good to have someone
like you jump to his defense."

Shayne looked surprised. "He ought to be glad to
have an autopsy. If we can find a few shreds of evidence pointing to a bad heart, or to a prior attack of
some sort—"

"That's exactly what he doesn't want," Dyer exploded.
"Don't you see the position he's in, Shayne, with the
Free Press riding him, and warning people to expect
you to pull a fast one? If the autopsy does show anything like that, no one will believe it. Towne figures it
would be a lot better to let it ride as a straight traffic
accident. He's legally in the clear on it that way. All the
evidence indicates that he was driving slowly and the
soldier either fell or threw himself under his car. He
stopped immediately and gave first aid and reported
the accident."

Shayne shrugged, and leaned back to cross one long
leg over the other. "Jeff Towne has changed a lot during

the past ten years if he won't pay out money for a cover-up."

"He hasn't changed, if you mean developing a conscience or something like that. A traffic accident can happen to anyone. It'll lose him a few votes, but people will think more of him if he squarely accepts the blame without trying to weasel out of it on a technicality."

"So he halted the autopsy?"

Dyer looked at him in surprise. "Did I say that? Towne doesn't run this department—yet. Doc Thompson's report should be ready any moment."

"How do you stand on the election?"

"The police department isn't in politics," Dyer told him. "Towne has the backing of the Reform Group, and Honest John Carter is backed by the *Free Press*. That ought to give you an idea."

Shayne lit a cigarette. "Towne might make El Paso a good mayor," he mused. "He's got enough money so graft won't interest him. He's honest enough—in his own peculiar way."

"He will make a good mayor," Dyer assured him. "Look here, Shayne, who the hell are you working for if Towne didn't retain you on this case? Somebody must be paying the bill, from what I've been reading about you these past few years."

"I'm taking a chance that somebody will," Shayne told him cautiously. "I suppose you haven't located Brown's folks yet?"

"No. That's one of the queer things about it. I wondered why you asked that question over the phone yesterday. James Brown appears to have been an alias and the Cleveland address a phony."

"Who identified the body?" Shayne asked abruptly.

"He had his dog tags on. We called Fort Bliss and a sergeant came down. The fellow had just enlisted the day before, so no one at the Post was actually acquainted with him, but the sergeant confirmed the identification."

"Check his fingerprints with Washington?"

Chief Dyer blinked suspiciously at the private detective from New Orleans. "You're holding out," he charged.

"Maybe." Shayne was noncommittal about it. "Did you?"

"The army is doing that. They took his fingerprints when he enlisted, and they've shot them in to the FBI."

"How did Jefferson Towne make his sudden jump to the top of the local heap?" Shayne asked suddenly. "Ten years ago he was a small operator."

"Guts and hard work and luck." Dyer shrugged his shoulders. "You know how a career like that rolls up. The *Free Press* is right enough about him trampling anyone who got in his way, but hell, that's the way men *make* money."

"Sure. It used to be rugged individualism."

Dyer nodded. "You were doing a job for him ten years ago when you were in town for World-Wide, weren't you?"

Shayne made a wry face. "It wasn't much of a job, and I didn't please Towne the way I handled it. Trying to dig up some dirt on a kid he didn't want his daughter to marry. There wasn't any dirt, so I didn't dig any."

"And he wanted some if you had to manufacture it?" Dyer supplied with a grin.

"Sure. That's why he was paying World-Wide. He took his daughter off on a foreign tour to make her forget the lad."

"Carmela Towne."

"Do you know her?"

"See her name and picture in the papers. His foreign tour must have worked, because she never married."

"I hear Towne's a mining and smelter magnate now."

"That's right. He first hit it lucky about 1935 with a mine in the Big Bend—just after the government upped the price on domestic silver. It's been a big producer ever since and he's bought up smelters and whatnot. I wondered," the chief went on reflectively, "why he was so damned sore about your horning in on this case. Didn't know he was carrying a ten-year grudge against you."

Shayne grinned. He was about to reply when the door was pushed open by a short man wearing a shabby and rumpled suit. He had a short-stemmed pipe clenched between his teeth, and his bristly mustache was yellow with nicotine. Waving a sheet of paper at Dyer, the short man said, "Here's your p.m. on that boy."

Chief Dyer said to Shayne, "This is Doc Thompson, and, Doc, this is the shamus from New Orleans who suggested you do the job."

Thompson put the report on Dyer's desk and nodded to Shayne. Removing his pipe, he said, "Shayne, eh?

You had an Irish hunch on this one, or maybe you bumped the lad yourself."

Shayne stiffened. "You mean Private James Brown?"

"Who else have I been cutting up these past hours?"

Dyer had picked up the report and was studying it with a look of incredulity on his naked face. *"Post-mortem damage,"* he read. *"Lack of ecchymosis due to extravasation, and absence of coagulation about the mangled area. Invagination of wound edges, lack of external hemorrhage,* m-m-m, *point to post-mortem bruising and prior death."* Glaring at Thompson, he yelled, "What the devil do all these ten-dollar words mean?"

"It's stated clearly enough," Thompson said. "The boy was dead before the car wheels passed over him."

There was silence in the office for a moment. Then Dyer ruffled the report, sighed, and asked, "How long before?"

"That's impossible to determine from an examination at present. However, I think you can safely assume not many minutes had elapsed. Certainly not more than half an hour, else the condition of the body would have been noted by Towne, or more certainly by the ambulance attendant who arrived very soon afterward."

"Rigor mortis?" Chief Dyer asked.

"Not necessarily. But there would be a noticeable, cooling of the body after, say, fifteen or twenty minutes."

"What caused his death?" Shayne asked.

"There's a head wound that didn't come from the tires of a car," Thompson answered bluntly. "It was incurred before the wheels ran over him, and caused almost instant death."

"What sort of wound?"

"Roundish. Half an inch in diameter. A single blow from a hammer would be my guess."

"How the devil did he get in the street in front of Towne's car?" Dyer exploded.

"That's your problem." Thompson walked stiffly from the room.

"This is one hell of a mess," Dyer said to Shayne. "You come along and ask for an autopsy, and now I've got a murder on my hands."

"Don't tell me it's unexpected," Shayne said gently.

"What do you mean? Of course I didn't expect it." Dyer got up and walked up and down his office fuming aloud. "Why should I suspect murder? It was open and shut. Now I've got this damned autopsy." He stopped to glare at Shayne. "How'd you get onto it? Down in New Orleans. By God, Shayne, you'd better come clean."

Shayne shook his head. "I've got to figure a way to make an honest dollar. Have you traced the boy's movements yesterday?"

"Only that he got a pass to come to town right after lunch, to finish up some unfinished civilian affairs. We haven't any further trace of him until Towne ran over his body at dusk."

He slumped down into his chair and fitted a cigarette into the end of a long holder. Shayne struck a match and leaned forward to hold the flame to the tip of the chief's cigarette. "It happened at the corner of

Missouri and Lawton," he mused. "What was Towne doing there at that hour?"

"He didn't say. It's sort of a blind corner, and the accident occurred just as he was turning onto Missouri, headed east. At dusk like that, he could easily run over a body as he turned the corner before he saw it."

"I think I'd find out who knew he was going to be turning that corner at dusk," Shayne suggested.

Dyer removed the cigarette holder from his mouth slowly. "Do you think it was planted there? So he *would* run over it and think he killed him?"

Shayne shrugged. "It pretty well knocks his chance of being elected mayor."

Dyer's fist pounded his desk. "With the *Free Press* backing Carter—and with Manny Holden making book on the election with even money against Towne—by God, Shayne, you may have it."

"Manny Holden?"

"A leftover from Prohibition," Dyer grunted sourly. "He's slippery as hell and back of most of our rackets. It'd be worth plenty to him for Carter's crowd to get control of the city machinery.

"It's a thought," Shayne told him cheerily. He got up and pushed his chair back. "Towne ought to be grateful to me for pushing an autopsy. It'll clear his conscience of the boy's death."

"He's going to hate your guts for it," Dyer growled. "Don't you see this is just what the *Free Press* hinted at this morning—what Neil Cochrane was preparing their readers for? Everyone will suspect it's the old cover-up."

"That's something else I'd inquire into," Shayne said breezily, turning toward the door. "How Cochrane guessed an autopsy would turn out as it did."

"Do you think Cochrane was in on it?"

Shayne said, "I'm just leaving you a few ideas to play with. Right now I'm looking for a client with a bankroll." He went out and closed the door firmly behind him.

CHAPTER THREE

A taxi took Shayne to Jefferson Towne's house on Austin Terrace, located in an exclusive residential section on the slope of Mount Franklin above the city. The address was not the same Shayne had known ten years before. At that time, Towne and his daughter lived in a modest five-room bungalow in Five Points.

His present residence was neither bungalow nor modest. Shayne sat up straight, and a grim smile tightened his wide mouth when the taxi turned under a high marble archway onto a curving concrete drive and circled across a terraced lawn to pull up in front of an ugly, three-story, turreted pile of stone.

Shayne got out, said to the driver, "You'd better wait. I don't think I'll be very long." He went up marble steps to a pair of heavy oak doors and put his finger to the electric button.

The left-hand door opened inward and a frock-coated Mexican stood stiffly at attention looking impassively at Shayne. He had a figure like Joe Louis, with the piercing black eyes and high, swarthy cheekbones of an Indian.

Shayne said, "I think Jefferson Towne expects me."

The Mexican inclined his head and turned and marched down a vaulted hallway with frescoed walls and a thick red carpet underfoot.

It was cold inside the big stone house, and there was an echoing, lonely silence about the hallway. Shayne's big shoes sank softly into the carpet as he followed at the man's heels. The Mexican stopped in front of open sliding doors and said gutturally, "Mr. Towne in here."

It was the library. Shayne could tell that by the rows of books along two walls. It had a low, beamed ceiling and the woodwork was dark walnut. There were dark leather chairs and smoking stands and a fireplace of Aztec tile at the far end of the room.

Jefferson Towne stood in front of the fireplace, with his legs widely spread and his hands clasped behind him. He was a big man, with a rangy frame that didn't carry any spare flesh even now after years of soft living. A man of heavy bones and whipcord muscles, seasoned by the Texas wind and the border sun. Tanned skin was tightly drawn on prominent cheek and jawbones, making his face a series of harsh contours. He had been a mule skinner and a prospector in his young days, and the look of those earlier days still clung to him.

He said nothing and made no move as Shayne walked toward him. He waited until the detective was ten feet away before saying harshly, "I thought you'd be out to see me."

Shayne said, "I'm glad I didn't disappoint you." He stood for a moment eyeing Towne levelly, and neither of them made any motion to shake hands. Shayne lifted his left shoulder in an almost imperceptible shrug, and turned aside to sit in a leather upholstered chair. Towne didn't move from his position on the tiled hearth.

Shayne said, "It looks as though you've got yourself into a mess."

"I didn't send for you."

Shayne lit a cigarette and grinned up at the big man. "I figured maybe you didn't know how to reach me."

"You had no right to tell Dyer you were acting for me. Demanding an autopsy of all the damn-fool things."

"I didn't tell Dyer I was acting for you."

"You gave him to understand I had retained you," Towne growled.

"He probably wouldn't have ordered the autopsy if he hadn't thought that," Shayne agreed tranquilly.

"Do you realize what you've done by your interference? You've given the impression that it's something more than a mere traffic accident. People know that a man of your reputation isn't called in on a case unless it's pretty desperate."

Shayne said mockingly, "That's too bad. I should be ashamed of having such a reputation."

Towne's dark eyes glittered angrily. "The whole thing would have died a natural death if you'd stayed out of it."

"I thought an autopsy was a good idea," Shayne murmured. "If we can find some evidence that the man was dead before your car struck him—raise a reasonable doubt—"

"But damn it, that's the worst thing possible under the circumstances!" Towne exploded. "Read last night's *Free Press* and you'll see what I mean. Your guns are spiked before you get started. Any testimony of that sort will be regarded as whitewash. Every voter will believe the medical examiner was bribed."

Shayne said, "I read last night's *Free Press*."

"Then you know how things stand. The best thing you can do is to get out of town and leave it alone."

Shayne said, "I was never paid a fee to stay off a case, but—" He shrugged and let the implication lie there before Towne.

"How much?" asked Towne bitterly.

"I don't know whether we can hush up the autopsy now," mused Shayne, frowning down at his cigarette. "With Dyer and Doctor Thompson both."

"What's that?" demanded Towne. "I told Dyer last night there wouldn't be an autopsy."

"He must have misunderstood you."

"Are you telling me it's already been made?"

"Why, yes." Shayne looked up in surprise. "And it clears you, Towne. The soldier was dead before you ran over him."

"No one will believe that," Towne snorted. "The *Free Press* will howl bribery and corruption. Of all the asinine stunts! If you'd deliberately planned to lose me the election, Shayne, you couldn't have done worse."

"The man was obviously murdered," Shayne told him dispassionately. "You wouldn't want to cover up murder, would you?"

"What the hell do I care how the soldier died?" raged Towne. "He's dead. All the autopsies in the world won't bring him back to life. No one even knows who he was, it seems. Probably enlisted under an alias to hide a criminal record. Lord, the *Free Press* will be saying next that I murdered him."

"So you *do* need me," Shayne pointed out happily. "The only way now is to find out who *did* murder him. You're lucky I'm available for a modest fee."

"Lucky!" roared Towne. "By God, Shayne, I get it now! You planned it this way. You fixed that autopsy to make it appear the man was murdered and force me into a corner where I'd have to hire you to solve a crime that was never committed. I'll see you in hell first."

"You have a filthy mind," Shayne reproved him.

"I know the way you work. You've planned a sweet shakedown, but I'm not playing. Get out."

Shayne reached out a long arm and mashed his cigarette butt in a smoking stand. He sighed, "I'm sorry you see things this way. I'm on the case now whether you like it or not. If you don't want to retain me—"

"Get out of my house," grated Towne between clenched teeth. He unclasped his hands and swung them loosely at his sides, balled into big fists.

Shayne got up and walked toward the hallway. He stopped in the entrance and turned to ask, "What were you doing at Lawton and Missouri at dusk? Was it a regular route you took, or did you have an appointment with someone?"

Towne glared at him and didn't answer. Shayne shook his red head reprovingly. "You're making it tough on yourself, Towne." He waited a moment, then turned and went out when he still didn't receive any reply from the Reform candidate.

CHAPTER FOUR

A man was lounging against the wall opposite Shayne's hotel door when the detective got out of the elevator and walked down the corridor. He had a thin, hatchet face, with a Panama tipped forward over it, and he was idly chewing on a toothpick. A pair of watery blue eyes watched the detective speculatively from beneath the brim of the Panama as he approached.

Shayne stopped at his door and put the key in the lock. The man straightened up and said, "Shayne?" as he opened the door. Shayne looked over his shoulder with his hand on the knob. He said, "That's right," and pushed the door open and went in. The man sauntered across the hall and followed him inside. He said past the toothpick, "Boss wants to see yuh."

Shayne had gone over to his suitcase lying open on the bed. He lifted out a bottle of cognac and unwrapped a pajama jacket from it, threw the jacket back into the suitcase, and set the bottle on a small table by the bed. He said, "That's fine," and went into the bathroom.

The man was still standing by the door when he returned with two water tumblers. He set one glass down and poured the other half full of cognac, then held the bottle out toward his uninvited guest, suggesting, "You'd better pour your own."

"Un-uh," the man said placidly. "Thanks jest thuh same."

Shayne nodded and set the bottle down. He moved back to a rocking chair and sat down, held the glass to his lips, and swallowed three times. He smacked his lips approvingly and said, "That hits the spot."

"Dintcha hear what I said?" the man asked in a troubled voice.

Shayne said, "Sure." He took another drink and set the glass on the floor beside his chair. He got out a pack of cigarettes and held them out. "Have one of these?"

"Un-uh." The man jerked his head. "Thanks jest thuh same."

Shayne lit a cigarette. The man took the frayed toothpick from his mouth and inspected it mournfully. He put the unchewed end back between his teeth and said, "Well, whatcha say?"

Shayne blew out a cloud of smoke and reached down for his glass. "Why don't you sit down if you intend to stay?"

"But I ain't gonna stay. You're goin' with me."

"Where?"

"Tuh see thuh boss," the man explained patiently.

"Who is the boss, and why doesn't he come here if he wants to see me?"

"People allus come tuh see Manny," he was told in a tone of mild surprise.

Shayne finished his drink. He laughed shortly and got up. "All right. I wouldn't want to upset the local routine." He went to his suitcase and fumbled in it, withdrew a .38 revolver. Without any effort at concealment, he slid the weapon into his coat pocket and went toward the door.

"Hey! Whatcha packin' that gat for?" The man backed away from him, looking frightened.

Shayne said, "My coat hangs better with a weight in one pocket." He followed the other out and locked his door.

"I dunno, but I don't think Manny'll like it," the man told him lugubriously. "It ain't friendly-like."

Shayne said, "We'll hope Manny doesn't feel too badly." They went to the elevator together and got in. On the sidewalk outside they walked three blocks in silence to the entrance of a small hotel which his companion indicated with a jerk of his head.

They went through a small lobby to a self-service elevator, and up to the third floor. The thin-faced man led the way down the corridor to a closed door, on which he knocked twice. It was opened almost immediately by a fat man in shirt sleeves. He had dimpled cheeks and a cleft chin and very small white teeth. He said, "I was beginning to wonder where you were, Clarence," looking past him at Shayne. His cheeks were pink and smooth and bulbous, and his eyes twinkled happily at the detective.

"I brung him, Boss," Clarence said. "But he's packin' a rod, Boss."

"A dangerous habit," Manny Holden told Shayne. He held out a fat, moist hand. "It was good of you to come, Mr. Shayne."

Shayne took his hand and dropped it. He walked past the fat man into the littered sitting room of a hotel suite. There were papers on the floor and highball glasses on the center table, together with a bucket of ice, a bottle of whisky, and a siphon.

Shayne said, "Hello, Cochrane," to an undersized man who got up hastily from a deep chair at the other side of the room.

Ten years hadn't added to the attractiveness of Neil Cochrane. His head was still much too big for his body, and a shock of bushy hair made it look even more so. He had a way of hunching his thin shoulder blades up and inclining his big head forward that gave him a vulturous appearance. His eyes were bright and ferrety and intelligent. He said, "So it's Mike Shayne again," and for some reason he laughed. His laughter was brittle, like the sound made by two pieces of broken glass being rubbed together.

Manny Holden closed the door and told Clarence, "That's all. You can wait in the other room."

Clarence went through an inner door and closed it, leaving the three of them in the sitting room.

Holden went past Shayne to the center table and asked cheerfully, "Will you have a highball, sir?"

Shayne shook his head and said, "Thanks." He asked Neil Cochrane, "Do you ever see Carmela Towne these days?"

Cochrane's thin lips formed an embittered grimace. He said, "No," and sat down.

Shayne pulled a straight chair around and sat down in it backward, resting his forearms across the back. He said, "Chief Dyer tells me you boys are backing Carter for mayor."

Manny Holden was putting soda in a glass on top of ice and whisky. He said, "I've got close to a hundred grand riding on him." He stirred his drink with a swizzle stick, and sank back into a deep chair.

"That makes the death of the soldier a lucky accident for you."

"That's right," Holden purred agreeably. "Until that happened, I figured Towne had a better than even chance of winning."

"But you were putting up even money he wouldn't."

"I banked on something happening to change the odds."

"Something like a soldier lying down in front of his car and getting run over?"

"Something like that," Manny Holden agreed. He set his glass down and folded his fat hands across his stomach. "And now you come in to pull one of your fast ones," he complained.

"It won't work, Shayne," Neil Cochrane said hoarsely. "I got a jump ahead of you by being in Dyer's office yesterday when your call came through. I don't know what kind of stuff you'll pull out of your hat on the autopsy, but nobody'll believe a word of it."

Shayne didn't look at him. He was watching the fat man. "But you'd rather stop the autopsy?" he asked him.

Holden pursed his thick lips and nodded. "Naturally I'd rather not have any trouble."

"Worth anything to you to keep it quiet that the soldier was murdered before Towne's car ever touched him?" Shayne asked gently.

Cochrane repeated, "Murdered?" in a shrill voice, but neither of the others looked at him.

Holden blinked his eyelids and asked coolly, "Is that the angle you're working on, shamus?"

"How do you like it?"

"I don't like it," he sighed. "Homicide investigations always stir up a lot of dirt."

"Somebody should have thought about that—before they planted a body where Towne would run over it."

Holden asked, "Can you prove that?"

Shayne shrugged his wide shoulders. "It's a reasonable assumption—as soon as we accept the murder theory. And Doc Thompson will make a good witness."

"I don't like it," Holden told him.

"It's one of his damned crooked tricks!" Cochrane blazed out. "Everyone knows he pulls that kind of stuff all the time."

Shayne glanced at him and warned, "You're not sitting too well. Your article last night sounded as though you had prior knowledge of what an autopsy might bring out."

"Nuts!" Cochrane shot back venomously. "I knew that's the sort of thing you'd try to pull."

Shayne said, "A jury might think differently—if I can show you knew Towne was going to turn that corner just when he did." He turned his attention back to the fat man. "How do you feel about your hundred grand now?"

"Quite well." Holden was unperturbed. "I don't think you're going to stir up a stink, Shayne."

"I'm open to offers."

"I'm not bidding against Towne," Holden said. "I'm telling you to get out of El Paso."

"I've got to make a profit," Shayne told him. "With a hundred grand riding on the election, you could afford to do some bidding."

"But I'd never be sure Towne wouldn't go higher." Manny Holden took a sip of his highball and added regretfully, "You'd better go back to New Orleans."

"How'd you like it if I twisted things around to prove that Towne killed the soldier before he ran over him?"

Holden moved his head slowly from side to side. "Things were going all right until you showed up. They'll be all right again as soon as you get out of town."

"It's easier to buy me off than to run me off," Shayne warned him.

"I don't think so. This isn't your town, Shayne. It belongs to me."

Shayne said, "All right." He stood up, his gaunt face inscrutable. "Be seeing you around," he said to Neil Cochrane and went out.

The door of his hotel room stood slightly ajar when he returned. He knew he had locked it when he went out. He walked casually past the door, glancing aside through the crack as he went by, but was unable to see anything inside.

He went on around the corner of the corridor and stopped. He took his time about lighting a cigarette, moving back to a position where he could watch the door. It stayed slightly ajar.

The incident didn't make much sense to Shayne. If

this was an ambush, the person inside his room was playing it dumb to leave the door open to warn him. On the other hand, he realized fully that he had stayed alive for a lot of precarious years by never taking anything for granted.

He tranquilly smoked his cigarette down to a short butt, then walked rapidly along the corridor, drawing his gun as he approached his door from the wrong direction.

He hit the open door with his left shoulder in a lunge that carried him well into the center of the room.

A woman sat in a chair by the window. She dropped a water tumbler from which she had been helping herself to his cognac. Otherwise she remained perfectly calm.

Shayne's alert gray eyes swiftly circled the room, returning to her face while he slowly pocketed the gun.

"Carmela Towne," he said in a flat tone.

Carmela pushed herself up from the chair with both hands gripping the arms. Her black eyes searched his face and she said, "Michael," making three syllables of his name, her voice throaty and a little blurred.

"Some day you'll get yourself shot," he said, and went toward her.

CHAPTER FIVE

Carmela Towne giggled, "I'm already half-shot, Michael," and held out her arms to him. Her lips were dry and hot and hard. Ten years had done some shocking things to her. She had been a leggy youngster with a rich, dark beauty that burned beneath the surface and glowed in her eyes. She had been vital and alive, tingling with youth and a fervid passion for life and love.

Now her long-limbed body was thin and taut, her face almost haggard. Two spots of rouge far back on her cheeks gave her a feverish look, and her eyes glittered with the same unnatural brightness. She was the embodiment of a woman who for a long time had made a habit of drinking too much, and sleeping and eating too little.

Shayne stepped back from her embrace, and she slid her hands down his arms to grip his fingers tightly. She asked, "Do you always come into your room with a bound like that?"

"How did you get in?"

"Oh, I bribed the bellboy. He asked me if I was Mrs. Shayne, and I told him I wasn't, and he seemed to think that made everything all right."

Shayne released his hands from hers and went back to close the door. He said morosely, "You spilled some of my cognac. It's hard to get nowadays."

"I'm sorry. I didn't spill much, Michael." She sank back into her chair, and got a cigarette from her bag. She put it between her red lips and looked to him for a light. When Shayne struck a match to it, she inhaled deeply and let the smoke filter through her nostrils. Tilting her head back to look into his eyes, she said, "It's been a long time," and for a moment forgot to be glib and flippant.

He nodded and extinguished the match. He moved back to sit on the edge of the bed and asked, "How did you know I was here?"

"I read the *Free Press*. And I know you were out to see Father this morning."

"At this hotel—I mean."

"You stayed here ten years ago. I took a chance and asked at the desk." Carmela made an impatient gesture with the long, thin fingers of her right hand. "Have you seen Lance?"

"Not for ten years." Shayne reached for the bottle of cognac by the bedside table and poured a drink. He didn't offer Carmela one. She didn't appear to notice. Her great dark eyes were fixed on his face. She said, "He's here."

"In El Paso?"

She nodded. "I saw him three days ago in a taxi downtown. He didn't see me. He was riding with a Mexican girl. A common little Mexican wench whom he must have picked up in Juarez on the *Calle de Diablo*. He looked terrible," she ended in a lifeless tone.

Shayne took a drink of cognac and murmured, "I've wondered what became of him." After a moment's hesitation he asked, "Did you ever see him after you came back from your trip abroad?"

"No. He'd left town. He never wrote to me, Michael," she answered softly, as though for an instant she lived in a dream.

"Why would he?" Shayne asked angrily. "Lance wasn't the kind to come crawling back after you kicked him in the teeth."

"I know." Her upper lip trembled, and a semblance of the fire Shayne had seen years ago kindled in her eyes. "I've hated myself for letting Father do that to me. But I was so young, Michael. I had been reared to think he was like God. My mother was Spanish, you know. She taught me that it was a woman's place to submit."

Shayne ignored the plea in her voice. He asked impatiently, "Do you know where Lance has been? What he's been doing?"

"I heard indirectly that he went to China. And later to Germany. Neil Cochrane called me once to say he had heard a short-wave propaganda broadcast from Berlin by Lance. I didn't believe it, but Neil later sent me a news clipping giving Lance's name as one of a group of renegade American journalists aiding Hitler."

Shayne scowled over a drink of cognac and was silent. The girl in front of him needed to talk things out. She had kept too much bottled up for too long.

"And now Lance is back in El Paso," she went on drearily. "He looks old and bitter and defeated. I thought you might be in touch with him. I thought that might be the reason you are here."

Shayne cocked his red head and said sardonically,

"If you read the *Free Press* you know I'm here to help your father get himself elected mayor of El Paso."

"That's not what he says." For the first time since Shayne had entered the room there was a hint of laughter in her voice. "You should have heard him raving this morning after you left the house."

"After I fixed an autopsy to show he didn't kill the soldier," murmured Shayne. "You'd think he'd be grateful."

"He knows no one will believe the autopsy. He'd much rather take the blame and have the incident forgotten."

Shayne said, "He'd make a better mayor than John Carter."

"I hope he's defeated," Carmela exclaimed passionately. "He's always had everything his way. He thinks he's a man of destiny. No one has ever successfully opposed him. Not for ten years. You don't know his cruelty and his arrogance."

Shayne reached for the bottle of cognac. He held it out toward her. Carmela relaxed and nodded listlessly. She picked up the overturned glass beside her chair and held it while Shayne poured it a quarter full. She drank half of it as though it were water.

"No one knows how I hate him. It's a horrible thing to say about one's father, but it's true. He's made me hate myself. I'll never forgive him for that."

"What do you suppose he was doing at the corner of Lawton and Missouri when he ran over the soldier? It's a block off the route out to his smelter."

"I suppose he was on his way to see that woman," she said without looking up.

"What woman, Carmela?"

Carmela lifted one thin shoulder in a shrug of disgust and drank the rest of the cognac. "There's a woman, in the next block on Missouri. I've known about her for a long time. Her name is Morales. He doesn't know I know, but I haven't cared what he did. She lives in a little house set back from the street with a high cedar hedge in front. I trailed him there once, out of curiosity."

"Does he go to see her regularly?" Shayne asked the question in a casual tone.

"Two or three times a week," she replied with hard indifference. "I don't think he has regular days, if that's what you mean."

"It is what I mean," he said harshly. "You see, Carmela, whether anyone believes it or not, that soldier *was* dead before your father's car ran over him. Murdered—and then placed in the street to be run over."

Carmela's black eyes flickered toward the cognac bottle. The tip of her tongue moistened her lips. Shayne poured a small drink and handed it to her. "So I'm trying to find out who might have known Towne would be turning that corner at just that time. Someone put the body there. Someone who wanted Jefferson Towne to run over it."

Carmela was turning the glass around and around in her hands, staring into the amber fluid as though it fascinated her. "Would anyone go to that trouble—commit a murder just to make Father think he had accidentally run over a man?"

"It's likely to make the difference in the coming election," he said. "And it might not have been a murder committed for that single purpose." He paused, then added, "It's a neat way to dispose of a body, to cover up a murder. It would have stayed on the books as a traffic accident if I hadn't horned in with an autopsy."

"Why don't you leave it the way it is?" Carmela cried out suddenly. "If you solve the case and prove that someone else murdered the soldier and put him there it'll clear Father completely. He'll win the election. I thought you hated him as I do. Ten years ago, you said—"

"Ten years ago," Shayne told her flatly, "I told your father what I thought of a man who would pay to have me dig up non-existent dirt against Lance Bayliss to prevent his daughter's marriage. My opinion remains the same today. But I've stumbled onto a murder, Carmela. Murder is my business. And I've got some money and time invested in this thing now. I've got to figure a way to collect a fee."

"I won't help you exonerate Father!" Carmela cried shrilly. "I'll see him in hell first. I hope whoever did it gets away with it and he doesn't get a vote in the election."

Shayne said, "You should have exhibited some of this brave spirit ten years ago."

Carmela Towne put her fingers over her face and bowed her head and began to cry. Her weeping had an obscene sound. It was as though something had rotted away inside of her, and her tears were a suppurating excrement bubbling up under the pressure of long decay.

Shayne got up and walked away from her. The

sound of her weeping followed him across the room. He clawed at his red hair and watched somberly, but made no move toward her and said nothing to halt the flow of tears.

His telephone shrilled loudly. Carmela took her hands away from her tear-streaked face to look at him as he strode across to answer it. Shayne said, "Yes?" and listened. His eyes narrowed and his gaunt features hardened. He started to protest, "Not right now," but he shrugged and replaced the instrument.

"He hung up on me before I could stop him," he told Carmela quietly. "It was Lance. He's on his way up here."

She jumped up with an abject cry of fright.

Shayne went to her swiftly and put his arm about her shoulders. He swung her toward the open bathroom door and gave her a little shove. "Go in there and lock the door. It might do you good to listen in at the keyhole and see what Lance has to say for himself."

She stumbled toward the door and went inside, pulled it shut behind her. Shayne waited until he heard the click of the lock from the inside, then went slowly across to open his door. He heard the elevator stop down the hall and let out a passenger, and waited to meet Lance Bayliss.

CHAPTER SIX

Bayliss would have been almost as tall as Shayne had Bayliss stood erect. He didn't. His shoulders drooped wearily, and his back appeared to be permanently bowed. His head was lowered, and he walked with a curious shuffle as though to balance his body with each step. Tendons stood out on each side of his neck, and he wore a shabby gray suit and a black bow tie about the frayed collar of a dingy white shirt. Ten years had thickened his torso and he looked well-fed, but his eyes held an expression of secretive wariness, and he seemed prepared to cringe should a hand suddenly be lifted against him.

Shayne put out his hand and said heartily, "Lance Bayliss!" After a moment's hesitation Lance put his hand in Shayne's. He didn't lift his head to look directly into the detective's eyes when he muttered, "Hello, Shayne. I didn't suppose I'd ever see you again."

Shayne kept hold of his hand and stepped back, urging him inside the room. "Come on in and have a drink."

He narrowed his eyes as he noted the manner in which Lance Bayliss entered the hotel room. It told him a lot about what had happened to the man during the past ten years. Lance came in with a sort of furtive

stealth, darting his eyes around in all directions suspiciously, behind the door and under the bed, and at the
open closet door and the closed bathroom door. He
kept moving toward the center of the room, and then
stopped to look back slyly over his shoulder while
Shayne closed the door. He said, "I guess I could use a
drink."

Shayne went past him and picked up Carmela's
glass and set it beside his own on the bedside table. He
split the remainder of the cognac in the two glasses.

When he turned to offer one to Lance, his guest
said, "I hope I didn't interrupt anything by coming up."

"Nothing important," Shayne told him pleasantly.

"I couldn't help noticing the two glasses," Lance
apologized. "You're not—married?"

Shayne said, "No," shortly. "Are you?"

Lance Bayliss shook his head. His hand trembled
slightly as he lifted the glass to his lips. He murmured
sardonically, "To older and happier days."

Shayne sat down abruptly in the chair Carmela had
occupied. He indicated another chair and asked, "What
have you been doing with yourself?"

"Nothing important. Bumming around here and
there."

"Writing any poetry?"

"Hardly." Lance balanced his glass on his knee and
watched it carefully, as though he feared it might disappear from his hand if he didn't keep his eyes fixed
on it.

"Too busy writing propaganda for the Third Reich?"
Shayne purposely made his voice harsh.

Lance Bayliss wet his lips. He didn't look up. "So you know about that?"

"Carmela Towne told me."

He winced at the sound of her name. "It was a dirty business," he said quietly. "I didn't think anything mattered during those years. I was being very cynical and disillusioned. The war woke me up." He lifted his eyes to Shayne's momentarily. "You've got to believe me," he said strongly. "I pulled out of it when Hitler marched into Poland."

"Since then?"

Lance shrugged. "Dodging the Gestapo mostly. I got to Mexico finally and ghosted a book there."

"What sort of a book?"

"Dictators I Have Known."

Shayne jerked to closer attention. "That was by the war correspondent Douglas Gershon."

"His name was signed to it," Lance admitted wryly. "I understand it sold well."

"It caused a lot of controversy. Half the people who read it found it pro-Fascist."

"It wasn't at all," Lance protested. "People felt that merely because it represented the dictators as human beings. They are human, and all the more despicable because of that. Hell, the book was banned in Germany and all the occupied countries." His grayish-blue eyes flashed fire at Shayne, then flickered away.

"Which might have been smart propaganda to get it more widely read over here," Shayne pointed out.

Lance Bayliss sighed and finished his drink. He set the empty glass down and said, "I can't prove it, but I'm on the Gestapo blacklist for having ghosted the book. I had to get out of Mexico in a hurry. You know what happened to Douglas Gershon," he ended hoarsely.

"Had some sort of accident in New York, didn't he?"

"They called it an accident. Gershon was murdered. I happen to know the Gestapo got him."

Shayne shrugged his indifference to the incident and said in a friendly tone, "What are you doing in El Paso, Lance?"

"Gathering material for a new book on Gestapo activities in this country." Lance's voice became animated and he looked squarely at Shayne. "It will include the true dope on some of our native Fascists who are either consciously or unconsciously collaborating."

"Isn't it dangerous?"

"I've lived with danger so much the last few years," Lance said slowly, "it's lost its impact."

Shayne took out a pack of cigarettes and offered them to Lance, who accepted avidly. Thumbnailing a match, Shayne lit both of them, spun the matchstick across the room, and asked, "Did you just drop in here to see me for old times' sake, or was there something in particular?"

"I wanted to see what kind of man you'd turned into," Lance told him coolly. "Your championship of Jefferson Towne intrigues me."

"He'd make El Paso a good mayor."

Lance Bayliss uttered an angry exclamation, and rose to stride up and down the hotel room. His words came in a rush: "That's typical of this country's smug way of thinking. Towne is a menace to the community and to America. He has the true Leader complex. Damn it, Shayne, don't you realize he sees himself as the Man-on-Horseback? The mayoralty of El Paso first. That's a stepping stone. A springboard to launch him into state and national politics. He's as dangerous as a Hitler. And you're helping him get elected by clearing him in a lucky accident that might have prevented his election."

"I don't think he's that dangerous," Shayne argued good-naturedly. "You're in the habit of looking for bogymen around every corner."

"That's the trouble with you here in America." Lance Bayliss stopped in mid-stride to level a trembling forefinger at Shayne. "You underestimate the danger. You sit back and say blandly, 'It can't happen here.' It can! It happened in Germany. You don't realize the forces moving us toward Fascism in the United States, with men like Jeff Towne eager to lead the movement."

Shayne said, "Perhaps," remaining unperturbed.

"There's no perhaps about it. Men like Towne have to be stopped before they get started. He *was* stopped until you stepped in with your talk of an autopsy to muddy the issue. You used to stand for something, Shayne. Have you changed so much in ten years?"

"I draw bigger fees than I did ten years ago."

"Is a fat fee more important to you than the welfare of your country?" Lance's voice trembled with wrath.

Shayne made a derisive gesture. "I can't believe the fate of one small city election is so important." He paused a moment and then added, "What would you have me do?"

"Drop the whole investigation. Get out of El Paso, and let the voters defeat Towne."

Shayne said, "A lot of different people are eager to have me drop the investigation. I'm beginning to wonder what all of them are afraid of."

"I'm telling you what I'm afraid of," Lance assured him angrily. He took time out to choke back his anger, went on in a more reasonable tone: "You've got to realize this is something big, and there are people determined to block you. You'll drop it like a hot brick if you're smart."

"And if I'm not?" Shayne's voice was hard.

"I won't be responsible for what happens." Lance Bayliss shrugged his thin shoulders. "Think it over. A fat fee from Towne won't do you much good in your coffin."

"That might be construed as a threat," Shayne mused.

"Construe it any damned way you want," muttered Lance apathetically. He went toward the closed bathroom door, asking, "This your bathroom?"

Shayne said, "Yes. Help yourself." He emptied his glass of cognac while Lance tried the door.

"It's locked." Lance whirled about suspiciously. "There's someone in there! By God—"

"It's a connecting bathroom," Shayne lied calmly. "Guy in the next room must be using it. Christ, fellow," he went on good-naturedly, "you need to quiet down and relax. This is the U.S. Remember? We don't have SS squads concealed in every hotel room."

"I am jumpy," Lance conceded with a bitter twist of his lips. "I'm sorry you're determined to be stubborn about going to bat for Towne. I guess there isn't much more to say."

"I guess there isn't." Shayne stayed in his chair. "If you feel like settling down to chew over other things, I'll see if I can get a fresh bottle sent up."

Lance said, "Thanks. No." He was edging toward the door. "Think over what I've told you. I'll be around and—"

The bathroom door swung open, and Carmela Towne was outlined in the doorway. She cried out, "Lance!"

He turned his head very deliberately to look at her. His gaze was impersonal and searching. He drew in his breath, and the small sound was loud in the stillness of the hotel room. He looked back at Shayne and said acidly, "I'm sorry I interrupted your drinking party. I'll get out and let you finish it." He went swiftly to the door and jerked it open.

Carmela swayed forward and cried out, "Lance," again.

He stepped out, and the slamming of the door echoed his name.

Carmela turned numbly toward Shayne. "Did you see his eyes when he looked at me? He hates me, Michael."

Shayne said evenly, "Ten years have taught him to hate a lot of things, Carmela."

"I heard everything he said. About Father and all. Do you believe them, Michael? Can they be true?"

Shayne said, "I don't know." He sighed. "I'm not even sure that Lance believes them."

Carmela came toward him slowly. Her features were

haggard and tightly drawn. Her dark eyes glittered insistently. "What do you mean by that?"

"I'm not sure." Shayne moved restively in his chair. "I'm only sure that Lance is trying to balk a complete investigation into the death of the soldier. Other people are trying to do the same thing for different reasons." He got up and jerked his head curtly toward the chair. "Sit down and relax. I'll order up that bottle and we'll pour ourselves a drink."

CHAPTER SEVEN

Early in the afternoon Shayne strolled down to police headquarters and went up a corridor toward Chief Dyer's private office. He was nearing the door when it opened and Dyer came out. He was accompanied by Neil Cochrane of the *Free Press* and a long-legged young man with tousled hair and a solemn face and round, wondering eyes behind a pair of thick-lensed glasses.

Dyer was puffing explosively on his inevitable cigarette in its long holder. When he saw Shayne, he told the two men, "Here he is now, if you want to ask him those questions. You can use my office if you like. You know Cochrane, don't you, Shayne? And this is Jasper Dodge, on the morning paper."

Shayne said, yes, he knew Cochrane. He shook hands with the solemn-faced young reporter, who mumbled that he was happy to meet Mr. Shayne. Dyer started to go on by, but Shayne blocked him for a moment. "What's this all about, Chief?"

"I just gave the boys a statement on the autopsy. They want to ask you a few questions. They want to know on what information you based your request for an autopsy, and who retained you on the case."

Shayne grinned and said, "The hell they do."

"And other pertinent questions," Neil Cochrane shot at him incisively, thrusting his bushy head forward. "My readers will want to know—"

Shayne said, "To hell with your readers, Cochrane. I'm not ready to make a statement yet." He linked his arm in Chief Dyer's. "I've a couple of things I wanted to talk over with you."

"Busy right now." Dyer started down the hall. "Boys have pulled in a couple of suspects on an angle we've been working on for some time."

"I'll tag along," Shayne said agreeably.

"Yeah. And we'll tag along too, Shayne," Cochrane grated disagreeably. "My paper wants to know who put up the bribe money that caused Doc Thompson to falsify an autopsy."

Shayne didn't pay any attention to the little man's yapping. He went down the hallway with Dyer, and the two reporters trailed behind.

"What sort of an angle?" Shayne asked the chief idly.

"Boys from Fort Bliss have been turning up in Juarez more or less regularly with civilian clothes for an evening's what-have-you," Dyer told him. "We've been cooperating with the army authorities—" He broke off to stop and open a door into one of the detention rooms just off the booking desk.

Shayne went in with him. There were two uniformed policemen standing in the bare room, and two other occupants were seated.

One of them was a young Mexican girl. She didn't look over sixteen. She had sultry eyes and a sullen, heavily rouged mouth. She wore a thin white blouse that showed a pink brassiere beneath, and a very short skirt that came well above her knees as she sprawled on a bench. Her rayon stockings were twisted, and one of them had a run all the way down the inside of her calf.

Her companion was a tall, dapper man. He sat bolt upright beside the Mexican floosie, with his hands folded in his lap. He had fierce eyes and a beaked nose, and a square, aggressive jaw.

"Here they are, Chief," one of the patrolmen said. "The guy won't do no talkin', but the girl says—"

She opened her mouth and spewed out a torrent of Mexican vilification at him. Her companion compressed his lips tightly and did not look at her. She ceased abruptly in the middle of a sentence, and her eyes widened as the two reporters peered through the doorway behind Shayne and Chief Dyer. She jumped up and cried out, "*Señor* Cochrane! You 'ave come for tal them Marquita ees not bad girl. You weel mak' them let me go, no?"

Neil Cochrane lounged forward with a sickly smile on his ferrety face. He asked, "What have you been up to, Marquita?"

"Nossing. I 'ave done nossing at all. Bot zees mans arrest me, for w'at I do not know." She shrugged her shoulders defiantly and wriggled her thin hips, then plopped herself down on the bench again, twitching her skirt above her knees and letting her mouth relax into sullen lines.

"How well do you know this girl?" Dyer demanded of the *Free Press* reporter.

"I've run into her in Juarez a couple of times. What are the charges against her?"

Chief Dyer turned inquiringly to the patrolman who had first spoken.

"We picked her up taking a couple of young soldiers in uniform into this man's secondhand clothing store," the officer said. "We've been watching his place for some time on the hunch that he rented civvies to soldiers who want to slip across the border for a good time. Couple of M.P.'s went in with us, and the soldiers said, sure, she'd picked 'em up on the street and offered to show 'em how to get out to Juarez without gettin' caught,"

"Who are you?" Dyer growled at the dapper man.

"I am Sydney J. Larimer." He spoke in precise English, forming each word carefully, his tone incisive and superior. "I have a legitimate business and I protest this outrage. I demand the protection of a legal advisor."

"What kind of a business do you run?"

"I purchase and sell slightly used clothing and luggage."

"And rent civilian clothes to soldiers who want to slip across the border?"

Larimer glared at the police chief. "I demand to be allowed to call my lawyer."

Dyer turned his attention to the girl. "How long have you been taking soldiers to his place to get them fixed up so they could cross the border with you?"

Neil Cochrane interrupted to ask reprovingly, "You haven't ever done that, have you, Marquita?"

Chief Dyer whirled on the reporter and bellowed, "Get out of here! Both of you!"

Cochrane backed toward the door, protesting, "Is this a Star Chamber? I just want to see that—"

Dyer nodded to one of the patrolmen and growled, "Put them out." He waited until the door was closed behind the two reporters and then ordered the Mexican girl, "Answer my question."

She was looking down at her lap. She shook her head and said sullenly, "I do not know w'at you mean. Me, I 'ave done nossing. I am theenk eet ees nice eef ze *soldados* can go weeth me to Juarez for 'ave fun, an' I am theenk maybe they can buy clothes for change from uniform."

"So you took them to Larimer's store, where you've often been before."

"Never," said Larimer tightly. "I have a legitimate business and—"

"How much does he charge to rent clothes to soldiers?" Dyer demanded of the girl.

She lifted her head and widened her eyes at him. "I do not know. I theenk I weel ask—"

Chief Dyer uttered a disgusted exclamation and turned to stride out of the room. To the patrolman at the door he said, "Have Sergeant Lawson get all the dope, and then release them. You made the grab too fast. If you'd waited until the soldiers actually changed clothes in the shop, we'd have something." Muttering to himself, he strode back to his office.

Cochrane and Jasper Dodge were lounging against

the wall in front of his door. He brushed past them and went inside. Following Chief Dyer, Shayne was intercepted by Cochrane, who stepped in front of him and said, "Look here, Shayne. I want some answers—"

Shayne put a big hand flat against the reporter's thin face, and shoved. He stepped inside the chief's office and closed the door. Dyer was seated at his desk fitting a cigarette into his long holder. His naked-appearing face depicted extreme disgust. "That's the way it is in police work," he said. "Have to depend on a bunch of incompetents who go off half-cocked and ruin things."

Shayne eased one hip onto a corner of the chief's desk. "Speaking of those two back there?"

Dyer nodded. "We haven't a thing on them now. And they'll be careful from now on."

Shayne lit a cigarette and blew smoke into a cloud already rising from a violent puff from Dyer. "Larimer appears to be some kind of a foreigner."

"He speaks mighty good English," growled Dyer.

"Too good," Shayne said. "Too precise and bookish."

"We'll have to work up another lead on the racket now."

"You could hold the girl," Shayne suggested to the chief.

"On what? Juvenile delinquency? There are hundreds like her in Juarez and El Paso preying on the soldiers."

Shayne's gaunt face was grave. He murmured, "That would be a logical approach for a spy ring. Getting young soldiers across the border with a girl like Marquita. I suppose there are still places in Juarez that go the limit."

"If there is any limit," Dyer grunted. He leaned back to peer at the redheaded detective through a haze of cigarette smoke. "Are you saying there's a spy ring operating here?"

"Could be. It's a good spot. Close to the border, where information is easily relayed overseas."

"What sort of information?" Dyer snapped. "What sense would there be in pumping a couple of privates? They possess about as much secret military information as a taxi driver."

"If enough of them do enough talking, things begin to add up," Shayne told him. "The modern espionage agent is taught the value of extracting minute bits of information from every source. Add ten thousand of them up and you may have something."

"Do you think they'd hire a girl like Marquita for that?"

Shayne shrugged. "Not as a Mata Hari, but as a decoy to get the boys across the border to the right places. It's just a thought," he went on easily. "How did Cochrane take Thompson's autopsy?"

"He choked over it," Dyer chuckled. "The *Free Press* is all set to tear it to pieces as bought and paid for with Towne's money."

Shayne said pleasantly, "Towne didn't like it either."

"I know. He called me after you'd been out to see him. He figures you're playing the *Free Press's* game."

Shayne grinned imperturbably and admitted, "Maybe I am." He stood up and yawned, "Any chance of borrowing a spare police vehicle to do some poking around the city?"

Chief Dyer regarded him quizzically. "Who *are* you working for?"

"Myself. As far as I can see, I'm the only one actually interested in how and why the soldier was murdered before Towne ran over the body."

"I've got men on it, but it looks like a dead end to me," Dyer growled. "Look up Captain Gerlach and tell him I said to give you the key to one of the homicide crates."

Shayne thanked him and sauntered out to look for Captain Gerlach.

CHAPTER EIGHT

Half an hour later Michael Shayne was rolling west on Main Street as it roughly paralleled the course of the Rio Grande out toward the smelters. He was driving an unmarked coupé loaned to him by Captain Gerlach.

He turned to the right at the intersection of Lawton, and drove the one block toward Missouri at about twenty miles an hour. The two streets met at an acute angle, and at that speed Shayne had to swing the coupé out in a wide arc to make the turn eastward onto Missouri. It was quite evident that the sharp corner could not be negotiated at a greater speed than he had been driving.

He pulled the coupé in to the curb and walked back toward the corner. Faint chalk marks still remained on the pavement, showing where the police had outlined the position of the soldier's body and had traced the tire marks of Towne's limousine around the corner. The chalk lines indicating the path of Towne's tires stopped about ten feet beyond where the body had been run over.

Shayne stood on the curb and studied the chalk marks carefully. Towne's heavy limousine had cut the corner more sharply than the coupé, indicating that Towne was driving at even less than twenty miles per hour, an assumption that was borne out by the fact that he had stopped within ten feet after running over the body.

The spot had been well chosen if the body was placed in the street in the hope of having it run over by a car rounding the corner at slow speed. The acuteness of the angle would prevent a driver from seeing what lay ahead until his car was fully straightened out. And at dusk, when headlights give little actual illumination, Shayne could see that it had been easily possible for a driver to strike a body lying in the street without realizing it until the wheels passed over it.

He went back and got into the coupé and drove along slowly, stopping in front of a little stuccoed house set well back from the street behind a neat hedge of cedar. He got out and went up a gravel walk to the front door and pressed the bell. The hedge extended past both sides of the house, effectually screening it from its neighbors.

A woman opened the door and looked out at him. She was about forty, with a well-kept figure for a Mexican woman of that age. She had pleasantly placid features, dark skin, and her cheeks were smoothly plump beneath high cheekbones. Her black hair was drawn back severely from a broad, unlined forehead. She looked at him with perfect self-possession and waited for him to state his business.

Shayne pulled off his hat and said, "Good afternoon. Mr. Jefferson Towne sent me."

She raised black brows until they made a straight line above her eyes and said, "I do not understand."

"Jeff Towne," said Shayne expansively. "Didn't he telephone you that I was coming?"

Her eyes were puzzled, and she moved her head slowly from side to side. "I do not have telephone, *Señor.*"

"I guess he meant to come around and tell you, or send a message. Anyhow, he sent me to have a talk with you." Shayne tried out his most disarming smile.

Her eyes were very dark, a soft, liquid brown. She stood looking at him with disconcerting steadiness and it was impossible to know what she was thinking, or if she was thinking at all. She was clothed with dignity and a stoic reserve characteristic of her race. For a baffled moment Shayne thought that Carmela must be mistaken with regard to her relationship with Jefferson Towne, but he made a move to step forward and said, "May I come inside where we can talk?"

She stood aside, then, to let him enter.

There was a small, uncarpeted entryway through which she preceded him to a comfortably furnished front room dimmed by half-closed Venetian blinds at the windows. The structure was of adobe, bungalow style, with plastered inner walls, and very cool. Small Indian rugs were laid before the restful chairs, and a few good pieces of Indian pottery adorned the sideboard and center table.

Shayne stood in the center of the room looking around slowly. The woman seated herself in a rocking chair and invited him to be seated. Her serenity was a complement to the quiet, restful appointments of the room.

"Your name is Morales?" Shayne asked.

"Yes, *Señor*."

"*Mrs.* Morales?"

She inclined her head in assent.

"Where is your husband, Mrs. Morales?"

"He has been dead ten years." She looked at him steadily. "Why do you ask these questions?"

"To establish the fact that you're the woman Mr. Towne sent me to see. You haven't admitted that you know Towne."

She lifted her shoulders in the merest fraction of a shrug. Her dark, smooth face was inscrutable.

Shayne sat down in front of her and said persuasively, "I'm a good friend of Mr. Towne's and he's in trouble. You can help him by talking freely to me."

She said placidly, "I do not think he is in trouble."

"Do you read the papers, Mrs. Morales?"

"No, *Señor*."

"Or listen to the radio?"

"No, *Señor*."

"Well, don't you talk to the neighbors?"

She shook her smooth, black head. "I go only to the market before noon. Other times I stay at home." There was a ring of dignified humility in her voice that pictured the ostracized life she lived for Jefferson Towne's pleasure.

"Then you don't even know that Mr. Towne killed a man just down the street from here two days ago?" Shayne asked in surprise.

Again she shook her head. "I do not know this thing, *Señor*."

"It was an accident," Shayne told her, "but his political enemies are trying to make it look bad for him. You know he's running for mayor, don't you?"

"Yes, *Señor.*" An expression of pain crossed her face but was quickly erased.

"He ran over the body of a man when he was turning onto this street from Lawton," Shayne told her. "We think the man was placed there by his enemies so he *would* run over it. I'm trying to help him by finding out who could have known he was coming to visit you Tuesday evening. Do you understand that?"

"I understand, *Señor.*"

"Was it his regular day to come?"

"Sometimes I know when he is coming. Sometimes I do not know."

"How about last Tuesday?" Shayne persisted. "You expected him that evening, didn't you?"

"I cannot remember, *Señor.*"

"Nonsense," said Shayne strongly. "If you expected him and he didn't come, you'd certainly remember it."

"Perhaps it is as the *Señor* says." Her face was absolutely expressionless.

"He's in serious trouble," Shayne urged her. "He may lose the election unless you give me some information."

Her lips tightened the merest trifle. She said formally, "That would be sad, *Señor,*" and she got up to indicate that the interview was ended.

Shayne got it then. She was afraid Towne *would* be elected. As mayor of El Paso, she knew, he would cease his visits to her house. *She loves him,* Shayne thought wonderingly. *By God, that's it! She loves him and she's afraid she'll lose him.*

He got up, reluctant to give up the quest for information, but convinced of the uselessness of further questioning. As he slowly turned toward the door, he noticed a framed photograph of a flagrantly pretty girl on the sideboard. The full, round contour of the face was that of a child, but the sensual lips and the flashing gleam in her dark eyes indicated a maturity far beyond her years.

The picture was without question that of the Mexican girl whom Shayne had seen at the police station, taken before her mouth had become sullen. He went toward it, saying politely, "This is a beautiful picture. It must have been made when you were much younger, but the resemblance is remarkable."

"That is my Marquita. She is a good girl, *Señor.*" There was fierce, throbbing pride in her voice. "Marquita goes to the school in Juarez and comes to this house not often."

Shayne murmured, "Your daughter? but she looks older—"

"Thirteen only, *Señor*, when she pose for it. I have one that is later." Beaming maternally, she went to the center table and shuffled through some snapshots, selected one, and held it out proudly.

Marquita was seated on a stone wall with her knees crossed, her skirt drawn down so that it almost covered her knees. She was smiling into the camera and her long black hair framed her face in two demure braids.

Shayne studied the snapshot carefully, comparing it with the larger photograph on the sideboard.

"A girl to be proud of," he said, and placed the snapshot atop the others on the table. "When did you see her last?"

"She comes on Sundays. On most Sundays she comes," Mrs. Morales amended.

Shayne started toward the door, stopped, and asked, "I wonder if I could trouble you for a drink of water before I go?"

"But yes, *Señor*." She went into the kitchen and Shayne turned back to the table. He pocketed the recent snapshot of Marquita Morales, and was waiting at the kitchen door when Mrs. Morales returned with a brimming glass of water. He drank it and thanked her, went out and drove away in the police coupé.

CHAPTER NINE

When Shayne stopped at the hotel desk to pick up his key, the clerk said, "There's a party here inquiring for you, Mr. Shayne. He's sitting right over there on that circular lounge."

Shayne turned to look at the man indicated by the clerk. He was an old man with deep-set eyes beneath shaggy brows. He had sunken cheeks, a weak chin, and a long scrawny neck. He wore a shiny black suit and was obviously ill at ease in the marbled grandeur of the Paso del Norte lobby. A dirty black felt hat was tipped far back on his gray head and he was sucking noisily on a short-stemmed briar.

After studying him for a moment, Shayne was positive he had never seen the man before. He walked over to him and said, "You wanted to see me? I'm Shayne."

"The detective I read about in the papers?" He came hastily to his feet.

Shayne nodded.

"Then I wanta see you, I reckon. Yes, sir, I sure do." He bobbed his head up and down several times as he spoke.

"What about?" Shayne made a move to sit down on the circular lounge.

"It's sorta private," the old man quavered, glancing

around the crowded lobby. "Couldn't we go out some place to talk?"

Shayne dangled his room key and suggested, "I've got a drink up in my room."

"Now, that'd be right nice. Yes, sir, I say that'd be right nice." The old man chuckled and held out a blue-veined hand, gnarled and callused by long years of hard work. "Name's Josiah Riley," he announced.

Shayne shook hands with him and led the way toward the elevator. They went up to his room, and he indicated a chair while he went into the bathroom to wash out the two glasses he and Carmela had drunk from. He came back and uncorked the bottle of rye he had ordered after Lance Bayliss left, poured out two drinks, and handed one to Josiah Riley.

"I take this right friendly of you," the old fellow told him. "Yes, sir, it's a real gentleman that offers a man a drink without knowin' what his business is."

Shayne sat down and stretched his long legs out in front of him. "What is your business, Mr. Riley?"

"I'm what you might call retired," the old fellow chuckled. "Yes, sir, I reckon that's what you might call it. Live by myself in a little shack on the river flats north of the College of Mines. Mighty pleasant an' quiet an' comfortable livin' by myself thataway." He put the glass of rye to his lips and his Adam's apple bobbed up and down until the glass was empty. He sighed gustily and licked his lips. "Got kind of usta livin' by myself back in the old days when I was prospectin'."

"So you retired after making your pile?"

"I'm not rightly sayin' that, Mr. Shayne. No, sir. I never made what you could call a fortune. Seemed like I had bad luck, sorta." He looked wistfully at the whisky bottle, but Shayne made no motion toward it.

"What brings you to see me, Riley?"

"Well, sir, I see by the paper that you come all the way up from New Orleans to help clear Jeff Towne in that there accident last Tuesday where the soldier got killed."

Shayne sipped from his glass and watched the old prospector thoughtfully and didn't say anything.

Josiah Riley hunched himself a little closer. His old eyes glittered hotly. "I'm thinkin' maybe you and me can do business."

"What sort of business?"

"I reckon you've done found out the soldier was dead before Towne's car ever run over him, hey?"

Shayne looked surprised. "What makes you think that?"

Riley waggled his head knowingly. "Maybe I got a reason for thinkin' it." He hesitated, and then went on in a querulous tone: "What I don't savvy is why Towne got you up here to stir up a stink. Not after he went to all that trouble to make it look like an accident. No, sir, I don't savvy that." He poked Shayne's knee with a lean forefinger. "Knowin' Jeff Towne like I do, I'd guess he'd want to leave sleepin' dogs lay."

Shayne reached for the bottle, and the old man held out his glass. Shayne poured a big slug into it and sweetened his own drink. He set the bottle back and said, "You know Jeff Towne, then?"

"I usta know him right well. Yes, sir, I guess you might say right well."

"He wants to be elected mayor," Shayne explained. "Running down a soldier at a time like this isn't a very good way to win votes."

"That's just the p'int." Josiah Riley waggled his head triumphantly. "Why'd he do it, then?"

Shayne's face remained expressionless. "It was an accident."

"That's what he hoped the voters'd think," Riley agreed. "Then I reckon he got scared an' called you in to help him out, hey?"

Shayne shrugged and asked abruptly, "What has all this to do with your reason for wanting to see me?"

"You might say it's why I'm here, Mr. Shayne. Yes, sir, you might say that. Jeff Towne's payin' you plenty, I reckon, comin' here from New Orleans and all."

Shayne said, "I generally get well paid."

"Yes, sir," Josiah Riley cackled admiringly. "A man can see that." He looked around the hotel room. "Livin' here in a fancy hotel an' all. Drinkin' mighty fine bonded likker." He emptied his glass and smacked his lips again. "And Jeff Towne's the man that can pay plenty. I reckon he'd put out big to win that there election, all right."

Shayne said, "I guess he would."

"Well, sir, I've got a proposition, Mr. Shayne. Yes, sir, a straight out-an'-out proposition. All I wanta know is—does the doctor say the soldier was dead before Towne's car hit him?"

Shayne shrugged. "The *Free Press* will be out on

the streets in a few minutes and you can read all about it. It isn't any secret. The soldier was dead, Riley."

The old prospector nodded his head and cackled happily. " 'Tain't no secret to me, neither. No, sir, I guess you might say I've known it all along. And Jeff Towne thinks that'll put him in the clear, don't he? Thinks he'll win the election now that he's proved his car didn't even kill the lad?"

"It looks that way," Shayne agreed. "How do you come to know so much about it?"

The old man wrinkled his face into a sly grimace. "That'd be tellin'. Yes, sir, it sure would be tellin'."

Shayne got up and put the cork back in the whisky bottle. "If that's all you've got to say—"

"Sit down, Mr. Shayne." Josiah Riley's voice no longer quavered. It was thin, but it had a harsh quality of command. "How much do you reckon it'd be worth to Jeff Towne to *stay* in the clear an' win that election?"

"You'll have to talk to him about that." Shayne remained standing with the bottle swinging gently from his fingers.

For the first time fear showed on Riley's face. "I wouldn't take a chance on talkin' to him." The quaver was back in his voice. "Not to Jeff Towne. I reckon it'd be better for you to handle it."

"What?"

"My proposition, Mr. Shayne. I'm an old man an' I don't want much. Two-three thousand, maybe. That's all I'm askin' to keep my mouth plumb tight shut."

"About what?"

"About what I saw down to the river last Tuesday afternoon."

Shayne eased himself back down into his chair. He uncorked the bottle and tilted it over Josiah Riley's glass. "What did you see down at the river Tuesday afternoon?"

"Enough to bust Jeff Towne's campaign for mayor higher'n a kite," the old man told him confidently.

"Exactly what did you see?"

Riley shook his head slyly. "You just tell Jeff Towne that. Tell him I was Johnny-on-the-Spot an' saw it all. That is, don't you go tellin' him who 'twas. He's got a fearful anger when he's riled up. He's liable to think he can shut me up cheaper'n he can pay me to keep quiet. Like they say in Mexico, '*Los muertos no hablan.*'"

Shayne tugged at his left earlobe and frowned at the old man. "*Los muertos no hablan?*" he repeated. "The dead don't talk, eh?"

"That's it," Riley cackled. "I wouldn't feel safe in my bones if Jeff Towne knew I saw what happened Tuesday afternoon."

"You're talking about blackmail," Shayne charged.

"Call it what you like, Mister. I don't want much. Say, three thousand. It ought to be worth that for him to get elected mayor."

Shayne said, "You'll have to put your proposition to Towne yourself."

"I tell you I don't dare do that. You're gettin' paid to clear him, ain't you? If I tell the police what I know, you'll never collect a penny from Towne."

"Why not?" Shayne snapped.

" 'Cause," the old man chortled, *"los muertos no pagan,* either."

Shayne considered that statement frowningly for a moment. His knowledge of the Spanish language wasn't extensive, but he did know that *pagan* meant pay. "Do you mean you have information that'll lead to Towne's death?"

"A man don't live very long with a hangman's noose 'round his neck."

Shayne said angrily, "You've been beating all around the bush without saying anything. What is the information you've got for sale?"

"All right, Mister. Here it is." The old man's eyes glittered venomously. "I saw Jeff Towne kill that soldier Tuesday afternoon. Saw him choke the life out of him with his own hands down by the river."

Shayne said, "You'd better tell the police what you saw."

Josiah Riley stared at him incredulously. "Ain't you workin' for Towne?"

"Not to cover up murder."

"If I tell the police, I won't get paid nothin'," the old prospector whined.

"Try the *Free Press,*" Shayne suggested contemptuously. "Neil Cochrane will pay you something for that information. And now you can get out," he ended casually.

Riley got to his feet. He licked his lips and started to protest further, but Shayne's uncompromising appearance stopped him. He went hesitantly toward the door, lingered there a moment as though he simply couldn't believe the interview was over, then sadly went out.

Shayne poured himself a drink when he was alone. He tugged at his earlobe with his right hand and went to a curtained window to peer out somberly. A newsboy was trotting down the street shouting a headline of the *Free Press*. Shayne couldn't hear what he was shouting. He went to the telephone and ordered a copy of the afternoon paper sent up. A sudden and enervating lassitude gripped him. He moodily went back to his chair and sat down to wait for the paper.

CHAPTER TEN

The Thursday afternoon *Free Press* was headlined: *Audacious Autopsy*. Shayne emptied his glass and settled back to read the front-page story.

It wasn't signed by Neil Cochrane, but it had been written by him. It began by reminding readers of the paper that the *Free Press* had fearlessly predicted yesterday that an autopsy would be performed on the body of the traffic victim in an effort to whitewash Jefferson Towne, and it went on at length to denounce scathingly the city authorities, who were being pushed around by an out-of-town shamus retained by Towne to do his dirty work for him.

It took Doctor Thompson's cautious medical report and tore it apart phrase by phrase, emphasizing the unreliability of such post-mortem indications, edging dangerously close to libel by broadly hinting that the police surgeon had been influenced, by Towne's position and wealth to make such a report.

Shayne grimaced and poured himself another drink when he finished reading the article. It was well written, and extremely inflammatory. The average reader would nod knowingly and mentally mark a ballot for Honest John Carter in the coming election. Shayne saw now why Jefferson Towne had been so worried about the result of the autopsy. From his point of view it would have been far, far better to let the incident go as merely another traffic accident. But was that the only reason for Towne's uneasiness? What about Josiah Riley?

Well, what about him? Shayne asked himself angrily. He didn't know. You couldn't tell about a man like that. If he was telling the truth, it appeared that Towne had a far stronger reason for avoiding an autopsy than the mere fear of losing a few votes.

Shayne closed his eyes and rubbed his chin reflectively. Nothing fell into a pattern yet. There were far too many bizarre elements that didn't fit in at all. Lance Bayliss and Marquita Morales and the proprietor of the secondhand clothing shop. Neil Cochrane and Carmela Towne and Mrs. Morales. Some of them hated Towne, and some were indifferent to him, and one of them loved him—and because of her love, hoped he wouldn't be elected. And there was Manny Holden with a hundred grand riding on Carter to win.

Shayne shook his head dispiritedly and poured himself another very small drink. There weren't enough pieces that fitted together even to begin to build a theory. Why in hell would Jefferson Towne murder a soldier? One who had been out of the States for years and returned to be met by a mysterious stranger in El Paso who persuaded him to enlist in the army under an alias. What had a boy like Jimmie Delray to offer a spy ring—or a counter-spy ring?

That spy stuff might have been all in his imagination, of course. Shayne had realized that possibility from the beginning. But why else would anyone induce him to enlist in the army under an assumed name? What could it profit anyone?

Jimmie Delray had written to his mother on Tuesday that he was going in to the city to meet the man who was responsible for his being in the army under a false name. A few hours later he was lying dead in the street where Towne's car would run over him. And Josiah Riley claimed he had seen Towne murder the soldier a short time earlier a few miles away.

Shayne laid the paper aside and stopped thinking about it. He stripped and went into the bathroom, shaved and showered, put on fresh underwear and the same suit he had taken off.

Dusk was gathering, not more than an hour and a half after Josiah Riley had left the room, when his telephone rang. Chief of Police Dyer was on the other end of the wire. He said, "Thought you might like to be down here when we bring Jeff Towne in."

Shayne asked, "Are you bringing him in?"

"Haven't you seen the *Free Press* Extra that just hit the streets?"

Shayne admitted he hadn't.

Dyer said, "You'd better take a look at it," and hung up.

Shayne put his hat on and went down to the lobby. A barefooted Mexican lad was passing out Extra editions of the *Free Press* as fast as people could grab them. Shayne glanced over the shoulder of an excited reader and saw a picture of Josiah Riley smeared over the front page. The caption read: *Murder Witness*.

Shayne didn't bother to buy a paper. He pushed his

way through the lobby and out onto the street. A copy of the *Free Press* Extra was lying on Dyer's desk when Shayne walked in. The chief of police looked up with a sour grunt and indicated it "Have you read that stuff?"

Shayne shook his head and sat down. "I can guess what's in it. Are you arresting Towne?"

"What else can I do?" sputtered Dyer. "Wait a minute!" He looked at the redhead suspiciously. "How do you know what's in the paper if you haven't read it?"

Shayne said, "Riley tried to sell me his story this afternoon before he took it to Cochrane."

"And you wouldn't buy it," Dyer scoffed.

Shayne shook his head placidly. "Why should I? It may be the truth."

"All the more reason why Towne should want it suppressed."

Shayne reminded him, "I told you I wasn't working for Towne."

"What are you after, Shayne?"

"I'm trying to solve a murder and earn an honest dollar in the process." Shayne leaned back and yawned widely. He was still yawning when the door was pushed open and Jefferson Towne strode in followed by Captain Gerlach of the homicide squad.

Towne's rugged face was purplish and he was fuming as he entered. "Damned outrage. Where's Joe Riley? I'll choke his story down his throat."

"He had an idea you'd feel that way and he asked for police protection after giving his story to the *Free Press*," Dyer told him.

Towne leaned forward and slammed his fist down

on the chief's desk. "The whole thing is a tissue of lies. What do you mean by sending men out to arrest me?"

"Can you prove it's a lie?"

"Of course I can prove it. Riley hates my guts. I fired him off my mine once for high-grading." Towne turned to glare at Michael Shayne. "What are you sitting there grinning about? Why aren't you out doing something? By God, this is all your fault! Without that damned autopsy, Riley'd never have thought up his outrageous story."

"Probably not," Shayne admitted.

"Here's Riley's signed statement," Dyer put in hurriedly. "I'll read it to you so you'll know where you stand." He lifted a typewritten sheet of paper and cleared his throat, then read aloud:

My name is Josiah Riley and I'm 78 and a citizen of El Paso.

I went fishing for carp in the river last Tuesday afternoon and started walking home about two hours before sundown. I was a few hundred yards from the river, walking along a little path through the brush, when I heard loud voices from a clearing in front of me.

It sounded like two men quarreling and I didn't want to get mixed up in it, so I started to go around through the brush and I saw a big swell automobile standing there with two men beside it.

One of the men was wearing a soldier's uniform and I didn't know him, but have since recognized

him as Private James Brown from a picture shown
to me by Mr. Cochrane of the Free Press. The other
man was Mr. Jefferson Towne, whom I have known
for many years.

I was a couple hundred feet away and they did not
either one see me in the brush, but while I looked I
saw Mr. Towne hit the soldier in the face and knock
him down and then lean over and start choking the
life out of him. I was scared of getting caught there
because I know Mr. Towne's awful temper when he
gets mad, so I walked on fast and didn't look back
any more.

Pretty soon I heard a car coming fast and I ducked
down and watched Mr. Towne drive past on his
way to town. He was alone in the front seat and I
couldn't see in the back, so I didn't know he was
carrying the dead soldier in the back with him so he
could put him in the street later and run over him to
make it look like an accident.

I didn't see a newspaper until today so I didn't
know anything about Private James Brown being
murdered, and I didn't think any more about it until
I read the Free Press.

I called up Mr. Neil Cochrane of the Free Press
because I knew they weren't afraid to print the truth
about even an important man like Mr. Towne, and
he took me down to the police station where I made
this statement, which is the truth, so help me God.

Signed, Josiah Riley.

Dyer looked up from his reading and asked Shayne, "Is that the same story he told you this afternoon?"

"Substantially." Shayne nodded. "With a few minor embellishments by Neil Cochrane, I imagine."

Towne turned on him slowly, his face working spasmodically. "What's that? Riley came to you with this story?"

"That's right," said Shayne easily. "He figured I'd pay him to suppress it—or hit you for the money. He only wanted three thousand," he ended gently.

"But you sent him to the *Free Press* instead. Without even consulting me."

"I'm not working for you," Shayne reminded him. "You told me this morning you wouldn't need me."

Towne doubled his fists and moved toward the redhead, muttering hoarse blasphemies. Shayne lunged to his feet, but Captain Gerlach got between them. The homicide captain was a big man. He shoved Towne back ungently while he growled over his shoulder to Shayne, "Lay off. He doesn't know what he's saying."

Shayne's wide nostrils flared. He said, "Sure, I'll lay off. When they kick the trap I'll be sitting in the front row laughing."

"Forget it," Dyer commanded. "It would have been paying blackmail to buy Riley off," he reminded Towne.

"Bring Riley in here," Towne said angrily. "I have a right to face him. He won't dare repeat those lies in front of me."

Dyer nodded to Gerlach. "Tell one of the boys to bring Riley in." He warned Towne sharply, "And don't start anything. I'll put handcuffs on you if I have to."

Shayne sat back in his chair and lit a cigarette. He didn't look at Towne, who now stood on the other side of the desk breathing audibly.

Captain Gerlach came back into the office, and Josiah Riley slunk in through the door a few minutes later. He threw a frightened glance at Towne and then quavered, "You said you'd pertect me. You promised—"

"Stand up and face him like a man," Dyer said. "Do you swear he's the man you saw choking Private Brown near the river Tuesday afternoon?"

"Yes, sir." Riley bobbed his head up and down emphatically. "I'll swear it on a stack of Bibles."

"He's a lying old goat," Towne fumed. "He's trying to get back at me because I fired him from my silver mine in the Big Bend for trying to pull a fast one. He's had it in for me ever since, and—"

"That's a lie." Riley's voice trembled, but he straightened up and looked Towne in the face. "I told you then it was a mistake. The kinda mistake any man can make. You didn't only fire me but you got me blackballed out of minin'. I never could get no job after that."

"You didn't deserve one," Towne told him coldly. "He was my superintendent in the Big Bend in 1934," he explained to the others. "He shut down the mine and came to me with a story about the vein being pinched out. If I had accepted his verdict, I would have closed down operations and later he could have picked up the property for a song and pretended he had found a new vein. But I suspected the trick and went down myself to investigate. You know the rest of it. It's been one of the biggest silver producers in the country ever since. Of course I blackballed him with every mining firm in the country," he ended contemptuously.

"It's a goldarned lie," Riley insisted wrathily. "I guess I did make a mistake about the vein pinchin' out. But it was a honest mistake."

"All that," said Dyer wearily, "hasn't anything to do with the murder you claim you witnessed Tuesday. Are you going to stand by your story?"

"You bet I am. It's the truth, that's what. I say it's the plumb honest truth."

Dyer jerked his head toward the door. A policeman led the old man out. The chief told Towne, "I'm booking you on suspicion of murder."

Jefferson Towne's big body seemed to shrink a little. "Just on the unsupported word of that old buzzard?" he asked hoarsely. "What motive would I have? If I did kill a soldier do you suppose I'd later run over the body and then immediately report it? Do you think I'm insane as well as a murderer? You know I jeopardized my chances in the election when I did that."

"I know all that," Dyer admitted. "I don't know the answers any more than you do. But the *Free Press* has forced my hand. If I don't put you under arrest now they'll make it worse than it is."

"Yes, I can see that," Towne admitted stiffly. He glared at Shayne. "That was your doing. Sending Riley to Cochrane!"

"You had a chance to retain me this morning—at a modest fee. I warned you that you would need me before this was cleared up."

Jefferson Towne tightened his lips and swallowed with difficulty. "I guess I made a mistake," he muttered. "You're retained now, and you can name your own fee. You've brought things to a point where we *have* to find out who murdered that soldier."

Shayne shook his head and said sardonically, "Hire yourself someone else to pull your chestnuts out of the fire."

Towne's face became suffused with anger. He doubled his fists again, but Captain Gerlach got in front of him and shoved him out the door.

Dyer looked at Shayne wonderingly and shook his head. "And he said you could name your own fee."

"I'm a fool," Shayne said bitterly, "but I never have liked to be cussed out." He got up and stretched. "I'll buy you a drink."

CHAPTER ELEVEN

Captain Gerlach stuck his head through the door with a big smile on his moonlike face and asked, "What's that about a drink?"

Shayne said, "I'll buy one."

"You're not in New Orleans," Gerlach reminded him. "We're pure in Texas. You have to buy it by the bottle and swill it in private."

"All right," said Shayne happily, "I'll buy a bottle and we'll swill it." He turned to Dyer to ask, "How about it, Chief? Closing up for the night?"

"Might as well—but I don't know—"

"Let's adjourn to my office," Gerlach suggested. "You used to drink cognac, Mike. How does 1912 Napoleon strike you?" the captain asked gently.

Shayne made a comical grimace and said, "I wouldn't dare touch the stuff without a physician handy. Where've you got it stashed?"

Gerlach chuckled and said, "Maybe we can pick up Doc Thompson." He led the way along the corridor back of Dyer's office, stopping en route to tap on a closed door.

"Who is it?" Thompson asked.

Gerlach opened the door a crack and said, "Bottle of brandy bites man. In my office."

"That I must see," the police surgeon answered

happily. He switched off the light and joined the trio in the corridor, looking suspiciously at Shayne over the sizzling bowl of his pipe. "It's the hot-shot again. I'm thinking Towne didn't get any bargain when he imported you to dig into this mess."

Shayne grinned and asked, "Did Towne kill the boy?"

"How should I know? The *Free Press* has him drawn and quartered for it whether he did or not."

The three of them followed the homicide captain another twenty feet down the hall to an office similar to Chief Dyer's, though slightly smaller. There were half a dozen chairs around the wall, but the three men waited in an expectant group while Gerlach took out his key ring and went to a square safe in the back of the room. Squatting before the door, he opened the safe, saying cheerfully over his shoulder, "This is where I preserve the evidence in important cases."

Groping inside, he drew out a bottle of aged Napoleon brandy, which he held triumphantly above his head. After closing and locking the safe, he stood up with the bottle dangling from his fingers. "Remember this?" he asked Dyer and Thompson.

The police surgeon stepped forward on his short legs to peer nearsightedly at the bottle. He whistled softly and said, "Didn't I analyze those bloodstains five years ago?"

"The Langley case," Dyer reminded him. "Mrs. Langley beat her husband's head to a pulp with that bottle."

"And not a crack in it," Captain Gerlach added, setting the bottle on his desk. He rummaged in a drawer for a corkscrew, and sat down to wrestle with the cork.

The others pulled up chairs in a semicircle around the desk. Shayne's gray eyes were intent upon Gerlach struggling with the corkscrew, but he asked Thompson, "How do you like Jeff Towne as a killer?"

"I like him." Thompson sucked on his gurgling pipe. "If I'd known what I know now, I'd have made that p.m. stronger. Hell," he added irritably, "I thought you were clearing the man, not hanging him for murder."

"I thought so, too," Shayne admitted wryly. "But that's beside the point now. The only thing I'm going to get out of this case is the satisfaction of seeing someone hang." The cork came out of the cognac bottle with a soft plop. "If Towne fits the noose," he continued mildly, "I want to see him wear it."

Gerlach passed the bottle to Shayne. After reverently sniffing the bouquet, he took a long drink and passed it on to Dyer.

Gerlach settled back in his desk chair and said, "There should be a handout from Manny Holden on this for you, Mike. Carter's election will be a walkover."

"That's the only thing I don't like about it," Shayne confessed, frowning. "I won't have done you boys any favor if Honest John Carter gets elected."

Gerlach nodded gloomily. "That's a cinch. He'll probably appoint Holden Police Commissioner." He took the depleted bottle from Thompson and poured down a stiff drink.

"The time element is the only thing wrong in the Towne set-up," Shayne mused. "Riley sets the time of murder about two hours before sundown. But you figured the soldier couldn't possibly have been dead more than half an hour before Towne ran over him at dusk."

"Not more than that," the police surgeon agreed, "else Towne and the ambulance attendant would certainly have noticed the condition of the body."

"Which throws Riley's statement off a couple of hours." Shayne spread out his big hands in an impatient gesture. "Leaving that out—conceding that Riley's estimate of the time was wrong, and using all of your leeway, Doc—what in hell was Towne doing during those two hours after he killed the soldier?"

"Driving around with the body in his car trying to figure out how to get rid of it," Dyer offered. "A man often gets panicky after committing a murder."

"Not Jeff Towne," Shayne objected. "He'd take murder in his stride."

"Where's your motive?" Gerlach demanded. "That's where the whole case bogs down, Mike. We'll never get a conviction without some sort of motive."

"Maybe not a conviction," Dyer interposed, "but enough people will believe it to vote Carter in as mayor."

They all nodded assent to that. Captain Gerlach glumly passed the bottle to Shayne, who nursed it tenderly as he asked Dyer, "Did you turn up anything else on that pair your men picked up today?"

"The Mexican girl and Mr. Larimer?" Chief Dyer looked at him in surprise. "Nothing important. Her name is Marquita Morales and she lives in El Paso, but spends most of her time in Juarez. She's just another juvenile delinquent. Larimer runs a straight business, as near as I can learn. You were right about his being a foreigner," he added grudgingly. "A refugee from Austria. Entered the country legally through Mexico in thirty-nine. Changed his name to Larimer and has been here in business ever since. Hasn't been in any previous trouble."

Shayne tilted the cognac bottle and with the mouth scarcely touching his bottom lip, let a drink gurgle in. Passing the bottle to Dyer, his gray eyes narrowed and he said, "Here's a hunch. Find out if Larimer has had any contact with a man named Lance Bayliss, an American citizen who recently returned from Mexico after dodging out of Germany ahead of the Gestapo."

"Lance Bayliss?" Gerlach repeated the name thoughtfully. "Isn't that the name of the young fellow who was sweet on Carmela Towne ten years ago—when Towne hired you to bust it up?"

"That's right. Don't ask me what I'm trying to prove. I don't know—but I've got a feeling we're only starting on this thing."

There was a moment of quiet. The three men looked steadily at Shayne, who absently massaged his earlobe. Then he said, "I've been holding out on you. I'm so damned used to holding out on the police in Miami and New Orleans where I depended on collecting a fee by staying a couple of jumps ahead of them, it's become second nature with me. This is one time when I don't have to."

Captain Gerlach leaned forward and folded his arms on his desk. Chief Dyer took the cognac bottle from his lips and hurriedly passed it to Thompson, rumpled his browless forehead, and glared at Shayne. Thompson set the bottle on the desk, untouched, and turned a humorous twinkle on Shayne.

"Well, what are we waiting for?" Dyer snapped.

"I first got in on this case through a little old lady in New Orleans—name of Delray." Shayne then related the details of his conference in his New Orleans office.

The chief's face grew red with anger as he listened. When Shayne finished, he exclaimed, "So that's why you wanted an autopsy! And that's how you knew the army wasn't going to locate his parents in Cleveland. Did you know they buried the body at Bliss this afternoon because they didn't know what else to do with him?"

"I didn't know, but I supposed that would be what they'd do. We've still got to keep it quiet," he went on emphatically. "It's our one ace in the hole. The killer, or gang of killers, doesn't know about the letter Jimmie Delray wrote his mother, and doesn't suspect that we know who the boy really is. They think they're clean. Towne's arrest has given them a further sense of security."

"If Towne himself isn't the killer," Gerlach muttered.

"That's right. If Towne isn't the killer. In the meantime, you can start digging for a motive for Towne to have killed a Jimmie Delray of New Orleans instead of an unknown recruit."

Captain Gerlach's telephone rang. He picked it up, talked for a moment, saying finally, "All right. I'll have a look."

Replacing the instrument, he said to Dyer, "That

was Sheriff Craven from below Ysleta. They've just pulled a man's body out of the river."

Shayne asked, "Isn't that well beyond the city limits?"

"Sure. But the sheriff says the body has been in the river for some time and may have floated several miles. That would put it in our jurisdiction." Gerlach stood up and put his hat on.

Shayne asked, "Mind if I go along?"

"Glad to have you."

Chief Dyer swore softly, and Doc Thompson chuckled as Gerlach led the way from the office and Shayne followed him with a wave of his hand and a final farewell look at the cognac bottle on the desk.

CHAPTER TWELVE

Captain Gerlach was a big, easygoing man who more than filled his half of the front seat of the police sedan. He switched on his red police light as they wheeled away from headquarters, but he left the siren off and cruised along at a moderate speed until they left the city streets behind them and were on the highway leading to the irrigated Rio Grande Valley.

Shayne had come to know Gerlach quite well ten years previously when the captain was only a sergeant, and they had run into each other a couple of times in the intervening years, so they had things to talk about as Gerlach pushed the accelerator down on the open road and got the sedan up to sixty.

By mutual consent, they avoided any discussion of the current case. Gerlach was a man who never talked much about his cases while they remained unsolved. A stubborn, plodding man without too much imagination, he was a strong believer in routine police work and generally made it pay dividends in the long run.

They talked about some of Shayne's cases that had made the headlines, and he told Shayne about his nine-year-old son who was already studying plane geometry; and then they were well down into the valley and a flashing red light was signaling them from the center of the highway ahead.

Gerlach braked down gently and pulled to a stop alongside a chunky man wearing overalls and a blue work shirt. He had a flashlight in his hand with a piece of thin red cloth over the lens. He leaned over the door of the sedan and asked, "You the city cop Sheriff Craven phoned in for?"

When Gerlach said he was, the farmer introduced himself: "I'm Deputy Sheriff Graves. Sheriff's waitin' for you down by the river. Got my own car here," he went on. "If you want to foller along, I'll go ahead."

Gerlach said that would be fine, and he backed up a little while the deputy trotted to a Ford pick-up parked beside the highway and turned it off the dirt shoulder onto a narrow, unpaved road leading south between small truck farms toward the river.

Gerlach bumped along the dirt road behind the pickup, leaving the farms behind and passing through an area of low swampland, and finally to a wide, clear space on the river's bank surrounded by willows, where the road led down to a shallow ford across the Rio Grande into Mexico.

Three other cars were parked in a semicircle, with their headlights shining down on a group of men squatting about the corpse.

A yellow moon shed blurred light through a haze of corrugated clouds, and when Gerlach shut off his motor, they could hear a pair of iron-lunged frogs protesting the intrusion in the willows beside the road.

One of the men beside the body got up and came toward them stiffly as they got out. He was a portly man with a bald head shining in the headlights above a fringe of gray hair. He looked like a small-town shop-keeper, but a sheriff's star was pinned on his unbuttoned vest.

He held out his hand to Gerlach and said in a hoarsely subdued voice, "Glad you came down, Captain. This is sort of outta my line."

Gerlach shook hands with him and explained Shayne by saying, "Brought a friend along for company." The three of them walked slowly through the loose sand to look down at the body of a dead man.

He was completely naked, and the body was hideously bloated and looked greenish in the yellow light of the automobile lamps. A heavy, sweetish odor rose from the body. Shayne took a step backward to avoid the odor and thrust his hands deep in his pockets and watched while Gerlach knelt with the sheriff and examined the head wounds that had evidently caused death.

They straightened up and stepped back beside Shayne after a few moments, and the sheriff drew in a deep breath of clean air and said, "Hard to figure how long he's been in the water, I reckon. Some of the fellows here have been guessing a week. They claim the alkali in the water keeps a body from rotting."

Gerlach shook his head. "Not more than three or four days, I'd say." He looked inquiringly at Shayne.

The redhead nodded. "Unless there's a hell of a lot of alkali."

"Anyhow," said Sheriff Craven, "that'd be plenty of time for him to float down here from El Paso."

Gerlach nodded. "You can send him in to the morgue

if you want, and we'll try to identify him. Fix him up the best we can."

The sheriff plainly showed his relief. He mumbled, "We haven't got much of a place for that kind of work." He turned to a boy of about fourteen and beckoned to him with a forefinger. "Come here, Pete, and tell the captain how you come to find the body."

The boy came sidling toward them, keeping his face averted from the corpse on the sand. "I—I was jest settin' out some throw-lines fer catfish," he stammered. "There's a good deep hole right up yonder above the ford, an' I fish here lots."

"Ever catch anything?" Gerlach asked.

"Sure. You betcha." The enthusiasm died in the lad's voice. "Like I say, I was settin' out my throw-lines tonight an' one of 'em hooked somethin'. I thought my floats wasn't workin' an' I'd snagged a branch on the bottom, an' I pulled in an'—an' there he was. God'l-mighty, I was scared. I run a mile 'thout stoppin', to where I could phone the sheriff to come quick."

"Was he floating when you hooked him?" Shayne asked.

"Not on top, I don't reckon. Leastwise, I didn't see him. Water's pretty deep there an' I use 'bout four feet of line off my floats."

Captain Gerlach looked at Shayne and shrugged. They went back to his car and he called to the sheriff, "We'll take care of fingerprints and all if you send him in." They got in and he backed around in the sand and drove toward the highway.

"What killed him?" Shayne asked abruptly.

"I'll leave that to Doc Thompson. He's been beaten around the head and there are neck lacerations that look as though he might have been hung by the neck."

"Young fellow, wasn't he?"

"I'll leave that to the doc, too. Around twenty-five, I'd say." He pulled up onto the pavement and headed the sedan back toward the city.

Shayne leaned back and lit a cigarette. "Naked as a jaybird," he mused. "That's a funny one. I've seen girls come out of the water naked, but—" He let the sentence die unfinished.

"Could have been swimming and hit something when he dived," Gerlach offered half-heartedly. He shook his head and admitted, "It's murder, Mike. Those head wounds didn't come from any diving accident."

"Maybe the murderer needed some clothes." Gerlach said, "Maybe. But I can think up easier ways of getting them."

"Stripped his victim to hide his identity," Shayne suggested.

Gerlach said, "Maybe," again, but his tone remained pessimistic. "Lots easier to empty his pockets and cut off laundry marks."

"Unless he happened to be wearing a particular *kind* of clothes," Shayne said in a peculiar tone.

Gerlach turned to look at him slowly. "What do you mean by that?"

"Just a thought." Shayne shrugged. "If he was a cop, for instance, and his killer for some reason didn't want him to be identified as a cop. Or wanted to delay identification as long as possible. It wouldn't do to just cut off the brass buttons. The uniform would still be recognizable as such."

"We don't have any youngsters like that on the Force," Gerlach protested. "Not any more. The army's got 'em."

"That," said Shayne quietly, "is what I was getting around to."

Gerlach puzzled over the matter for a moment, then said, "I'm beginning to get you. You're guessing he was a soldier and was stripped of everything so we wouldn't know it when his body turned up."

Shayne said again, "It's a thought. A soldier's clothes are issue all the way down to underwear and socks. And as you say, there aren't too many men of his age out of the army nowadays."

"It is an angle," Gerlach agreed. "It's the only one that makes sense. I'll call Fort Bliss and check on any missing soldiers as soon as I get in."

"If we're right, that makes two of them in a few days."

A thoughtful frown creased Gerlach's pudgy face. "Maybe that spy talk isn't so wild, after all, Mike."

"How do you mean?" Shayne asked.

"That stuff the boy wrote to his mother in New Orleans. Look—did he say it was the *spies* that got him to enlist under an alias, or some undercover outfit trying to catch some spies?"

Shayne shook his head and said slowly, "I don't think Jimmie Delray himself knew when he wrote that letter. In fact, I think he was doing some wishful guessing about the whole thing. Maybe it was just his imagination, and enlisting under an alias didn't have any connection with spying at all, but he simply hoped it did to clear him of a feeling of guilt because he'd stayed out of the country all these years while it was at war."

"I'm not so sure he didn't know what he was talking about," Gerlach argued. "The FBI and Army Intelligence have been pretty active around El Paso. There was a good organization already set up here for getting stuff back and forth across the border before the war ever started."

"Smuggling?"

"Sure. We've always had more or less of that. Dope and anything else with a high import tax."

"Would Manny Holden have been in on that organization?"

"If there was a crooked dollar to be made, Manny was in on it," Gerlach assured him cheerfully. "And now that you've thrown the election to Carter, we'll never be able to touch Manny."

Shayne sighed. He admitted, "Much as I hate Towne's guts, I'm sorry I've put him on the spot."

They were approaching the lights of the city. Captain Gerlach slowed to the municipal speed limit and asked, "Where shall I drop you?"

"At the police garage if you don't mind." Shayne felt his pocket and nodded. "I've still got the key to that crate you loaned me today. Mind if I take it out again?"

Gerlach told him he didn't mind, that he would be happy to have the detective keep the key and use the coupé as he wished while he was in the city.

Shayne grinned and thanked him. "It's not bad to be

on the legal side of the fence for once," he admitted.

He got out when the captain pulled up in front of the police garage, and hesitated for a moment "Mind if I make a suggestion?"

"Let's have it."

"When Thompson looks over that body from the river, have him check the head wounds closely to see if he finds one corresponding with the hammer blow that killed the soldier."

The homicide captain nodded. "You think they tie together?"

Shayne said morosely, "I think we'll know more about it when we find out if there's another soldier missing." He went in the garage and wheeled the coupé out and drove off in the direction of Jefferson Towne's house on the slope of Mount Franklin.

CHAPTER THIRTEEN

The police coupé was laboring up the slope a block from the arched entrance to Towne's estate when the lights of a parked car blinked on from a point just this side of the driveway. Shayne eased up on his accelerator and heard the motor of the parked car roar into life. The headlights turned sharply onto the pavement, and the car rolled toward him.

They passed in about the middle of the block. Shayne had his spotlight off, but he kept it trained on the front seat of the other car as they approached.

He flashed the spotlight on momentarily as they passed each other, and caught a brief glimpse of the other driver alone in the car. He blinked the spot off and kept driving. He rolled past the arched entrance without slacking speed, watching the taillight of the other car in his rearview mirror. It continued down the hill toward town.

The face he had seen in the brief glare of the police spotlight was that of Lance Bayliss, crouching behind the steering-wheel and staring straight ahead, a pinched look of anger on his features.

Feeling quite certain that Lance had not recognized him as they passed, Shayne nevertheless took the precaution of driving around the block before turning into the curving driveway leading to Towne's house.

The lower windows were dark, but there were lights on the second floor. Shayne looked at his watch as he cut off the motor. It was a little after eleven o'clock. He got out and went up to the front door and put his finger on the electric button. The ringing of the chimes sounded sepulchral and far away.

Nothing happened for fully two minutes. He kept his finger patiently on the button, and finally a night light came on over his head. He took his finger from the button when he heard a bolt being withdrawn inside.

One of the doors opened inward a few inches, and Carmela's husky voice called out, "Who is it?"

"Mike Shayne." He pushed against the door, but a chain held it. Carmela said, "Michael!" sobbing out his name in three syllables, and the chain rattled free. He stepped inside, where the big hallway was dimly lit by a single bulb in a wall bracket.

Carmela's arms were tightly around his neck before he could turn to look at her. She pressed her long body against him and pulled his face down to hers. Her body trembled and her lips were dry and cold, and a strong odor of whisky was on her breath. She wore a quilted dressing gown and her hair was brushed back from her face.

She pressed her lips against Shayne's and they soft-ened and became warm. He put his arms around her and his hands felt the hard outline of backbone and rib structure beneath the quilted robe.

When she took her arms from his neck she said, "I've been waiting for you to come, Michael." She closed the door and threw the bolt, took Shayne's hand, and led him along the hallway toward a wide stairway. "I'm all alone and was waiting for you," she said again. "I gave the servants a night off after I found out—Father wouldn't be home."

She started up the stairway. She didn't look at him again, but hurried up the steps as though there was little time.

Shayne hurried beside her, his big hand tightly clutched in hers. Here in her home, seeing her dressed as she was, he was more fully aware of the change ten years had made in her. She looked older than her years, and he wondered what she had been doing since she deserted the only man she would ever love.

They reached the top of the stairway, and she turned through curtained glass doors into a sitting room which was thickly carpeted from wall to wall and lighted with one tall floor lamp by the side of a silk-covered chaise longue. The room was done in pastel shades, cream and pink. It didn't match Carmela's temperament. It fitted the girl he had known ten years ago, before her father sent her off to Europe, a pathetic reminder of all the things Carmela Towne had been. He knew she had clung desperately to the soft beauty of her suite here on the second floor of the ugly stone house just as she had tried to cling to the love that had been denied her.

Shayne had a sour taste in his mouth as he looked around and let his gaze finally come to rest upon a low lacquered table beside the chaise longue gleaming in a circle of illumination from the floor lamp.

Hammered silver ice tongs lay beside a silver ice bucket. There was an uncorked bottle of Scotch and a silver siphon, and a tall glass held two inches of the amber liquid with three partially melted ice cubes floating in it. An ashtray was almost filled with half-smoked cigarettes, and a second glass, unused, stood behind the ice bucket.

Carmela had stopped beside him just inside the doorway, her fingers still clutching his hand. She looked defiant and determined, as she said suddenly, "I need another drink—and you need one, too, Michael." She let go of his hand and went to the low table beside the lounge.

Shayne stood where he was and watched her put ice cubes and whisky in the empty glass, then splash soda into it. He felt sorry as hell for Carmela Towne.

She had sent the servants away and settled herself here with whisky and cigarettes to wait. He didn't think she had expected him. Now she was through waiting. Everything she did, every intonation of her voice, told of her defiant resolve to wait no longer for Lance Bayliss.

Yet he had just seen Lance drive away from the house. He remembered how Lance had looked at her in the hotel room that day, and he felt sorrier than ever for her.

She poured more whisky into her glass, sat down on the lounge, and beckoned to him, holding out the freshly filled glass. He went across and took it from her. She brushed her long hair back from her face and said, "I must look a perfect fright."

Shayne said gravely, "You look very attractive."

She trembled a little and put her hand on his arm. She said, "I'm glad—I want to look attractive for you, Michael. You see—I hoped you would—be nice—to me," she ended in a nervous stammering voice.

She looked up at him and smiled, but her eyes were miserable. Shayne bent down and kissed her lips lightly, He said, "We've got all night. You're not quite drunk yet."

She said, "No," and laughed. "Drinking does help, though, doesn't it?"

Shayne took a long drink, set his glass on the table, and pulled up an ottoman and sat down. A silver cigarette box stood open on the table. He took two cigarettes from it and reached a long arm out to put one between her lips. She lay back and watched with half-closed eyes as he struck a match. After he put the flame to her cigarette she said softly, "I've been lonely, Michael. So damned lonely."

He asked abruptly, "How did your father take the news tonight?"

"I wasn't here when they came for him." She pushed herself up with both hands on the arms of the lounge. "Don't tell me," she said drearily, "you came here just to talk about Father and the case, Michael."

"Was that all Lance wanted tonight?"

She winced, and her black eyes widened to stare at him. "What do you mean?"

"You know what I mean, Carmela."

She said vehemently, "I haven't seen Lance—since today in your hotel room. You saw how he looked at me then. He hates me. He thought he had caught us having an assignation."

"I met Lance driving away as I came up." She lowered her eyes until her long black lashes veiled them. "You're mistaken," she said. "Lance hasn't been here. No one has been here. I waited—" She reached for her glass and emptied it without opening up her eyes, set it on the table, and folded her hands laxly in her lap.

"What do you think of Josiah Riley's story?"

She twisted her mouth bitterly. "Do we have to talk about that?"

"I've got it on my mind," Shayne confessed. "It'll stay on my mind until you've answered a few questions—and I don't want anything else on my mind when I kiss you again."

"Are you going to kiss me?"

"Let's talk about Josiah Riley first. Do you know him?"

She moved restively. "I used to know him quite well. Pour me another drink, Michael."

He put ice and a lot of whisky in her glass, and a little soda. He put the glass in her outstretched hand.

"When he was working for your father?" he prompted.

"Yes. Just a little while before I went to Europe. I remember when he reported to Father that the vein had mined out, and how low Father was. And how angry he got when he investigated personally and discovered Joe Riley was mistaken." She drank half the whisky from her glass and relaxed against the cushions.

"Do you think it was an honest mistake?"

"I think so. Father didn't. He was convinced that

Joe hoped he would abandon the property so he could later buy it cheaply and pretend to rediscover the vein."

"That has been done," Shayne agreed.

"But not by men like Joe Riley." She opened her eyes wide, but her voice was thick and lifeless. "I'm sure he was honest in his report."

"All the more reason for Joe to hate your father for ruining him in the mining business."

"He does hate Father. He has never tried to hide that."

"What about his accusation today?" Shayne persisted. "What do you make of it?"

Carmela mumbled, "I don't know. What does it matter what I think?" She lifted her head and finished the last of the whisky, carefully set the glass on the table, and fell back inert. "I'm getting drunk. Really drunk, Michael. I've never done that with any man before. I've always been afraid I'd act awful. You won't mind, will you? If I get drunk and awful?"

Shayne said, "I won't mind."

"It's good to just—let go." Her black eyes were wide and staring again, covered with a film of tears. "I've held in—too long. I've always thought—"

"That Lance might come back?" Shayne supplied.

She nodded, closing her eyes and forcing two tears onto her thin cheeks. "I've been an awful fool, Michael."

"You were a fool ten years ago."

"And I've been one ever since." She pulled herself up with an effort, and cried wildly, "I've kept myself for *him!* Do you know what that means? Do you know what it means to be a woman of thirty? I'm getting drab. I've dried up inside," she ended, and the room rang with her loud, angry laughter.

Shayne said quietly, "You've got a lot of years left, Carmela."

Hysteria was added to her laughter. Her eyes were dry now, and shone with an unnatural glitter. "Not as many years as you think. Men aren't attracted to old women. Look at you! What do you do? You sit there and argue. If I were a luscious blonde of eighteen, you'd be kissing me. Don't deny it. You know you would."

Shayne said grimly, "We're still transacting business, Carmela. I told you I wanted to get the business over with first. Take a look at this." He reached in his pocket for the snapshot of Marquita Morales and showed it to her. "Have you ever seen this girl before?"

She glanced at it indifferently, then with intent speculation. "It's the girl who was with Lance in the taxi that day," she began in a low, harsh voice that rose to a shrill pitch as she went on, "That's what I mean! She's young and pretty! If she were here alone with you, I'll bet you wouldn't be sitting at arm's length from her. Would you? Well—would you?" She was sitting upright, swaying a little, and pointing a long thin forefinger at him.

Shayne sighed and replaced the snapshot in his pocket. "You were going to get drunk, remember?" He fixed another drink and put it in her hand.

She took a long drink and sat back listlessly. "I remember. I warned you, didn't I, that I might be awful?"

He said, "You warned me." The whisky bottle was almost empty. He put the stopper in the bottle and walked around to lean over her and look down into her upturned eyes. "You've got plenty on the ball, Carmela. Haven't you ever heard that the best years of a woman's life are the thirties? I'm going to kiss you, and you're going to discover that everything is all right. You're beautiful as hell, Carmela. Don't ever start doubting that."

Her eyes held his steadily. Her lips were thinned against her teeth. He bent his head and kissed her. A shudder rippled over her taut body, and she went limp. With his mouth still close to hers he said, "See what I mean?"

She touched his gaunt cheek with her fingers and pushed him away. Carefully setting her half-filled glass on the table, she looked up at him with glazed and staring eyes. "Help me—I'm so tired," she whimpered.

"Sure, Carmela," he said gently, and his eyes were bleak. He moved around and sat on the edge of the chaise longue beside her. Carmela's head rolled back, and she closed her eyes. A little moan carried from her moist red lips. Then she sighed convulsively and lay very still.

Shayne got up slowly and stood looking down at her. The muscles in his face were set, and he drew in a long, rasping breath. Carmela Towne didn't stir under his gaze.

He picked up her glass and drank the rest of her drink, then strolled across the sitting room to a closed door. Opening it, he found a light switch on the wall.

He pushed the switch and flooded Carmela's bedroom with light

He went back and gathered her up in his arms and
carried her through the doorway. She was very light in
his arms, and one of her furred mules slipped off and
fell to the carpet. Easing her down on one side of the
double bed, he turned back the covers on the other,
then placed her on the sheet. He hesitated before un-
tying the belt of her quilted gown and gently slipping
it off.

She lay quiescent and breathed evenly. He pulled
the covers over her and went out, closing the bedroom
door.

He left the floor lamp burning in her sitting room
and went downstairs. The front door was equipped
with an inner bolt and a chain, a heavy lock with a night
latch. He checked the night latch to see that it was on,
then went out and pulled the door shut.

Most of the city of El Paso was stretched out below
the front steps of Jefferson Towne's house. The glitter
of moonlight on water made a winding serpentine of
the Rio Grande, with a cluster of yellow lights on the
other side marking the Mexican city of Juarez.

Shayne sighed, and went down the marble steps to
his coupé. He got in and drove away without looking
back, idly wondering what he might have done had Carmela remained conscious. Given a chance at happiness,
she could be a damnably attractive woman. He recalled
his light words to Lucy Hamilton before he left New
Orleans for El Paso, and made a sour grimace.

He had never felt as sorry for any woman as he did
right now for Carmela, nor as disgusted with any man
as he was with Lance Bayliss. He wondered if Lance
had been in the house before he arrived, or if he had
merely sat in his parked car without making his pres-
ence known.

He was a fool for considering Lance Bayliss at all,
and was disgusted with himself and ready to go back to
New Orleans where he belonged when he parked the
coupé in the hotel garage and went up to his room.

CHAPTER FOURTEEN

Shayne read the morning paper with his breakfast in the coffee shop downstairs. It gave a full and fair account of Josiah Riley's accusation and Jefferson Towne's arrest, pointing out the discrepancy in time between the struggle Riley had purportedly witnessed and the time when Towne's automobile ran over the body, and giving a full account of the bad blood between the two men without pointing out that this might be a motive for Riley to falsify what he had claimed to see on Tuesday afternoon.

On the second page there was a gruesome photograph of the corpse that had been fished out of the Rio Grande the preceding night. To make the morning edition, the newspaper photographer hadn't had time to wait for the body to be fixed up any, and the bloated features in the picture were hardly distinguishable as those of a man. A complete description of the body was given, however, and the public was urged to view the remains at the city morgue that afternoon to try to identify the dead man. The news story did not venture any speculations as to why the body was stripped of all its clothing, nor was there any hint of a possible connection between the two deaths.

Shayne left the paper folded on the table when he finished breakfast. He found Chief Dyer in his office at headquarters, and the chief didn't appear happy. He greeted the detective with a surly grunt. "Why do you private dicks always try to complicate things?"

Shayne grinned and asked him what he meant.

"Trying to find a tie-up between an open-and-shut murder and an unidentified body," Dyer snarled. "Spy rings and so on! Gerlach says you told him to look for a similar head wound on this new body. Good God, Shayne, do you think Towne's gone in for wholesale murder?"

"What does Thompson say about it?"

"He says 'No.' There are neck abrasions, but death came from being beaten over the head with some blunt instrument. *Not* a single blow with a hammer."

Shayne shrugged. "That would have made it too easy," he admitted. "How long does Thompson give him in the water?"

Chief Dyer scowled, and waved his cigarette in its long holder. "You know how a medico is. With a lot of hedging and buts and maybes—from two to five days, and be damned if he'll set it any closer."

Shayne said, "Knowing the flow of the river, we can figure out some limits as to where the body could have been thrown in."

Dyer shook his head. "I tried him on that, too. Nothing doing. Some bodies sink to the bottom and lie there for days. Others never sink at all. That's no good."

"Located any missing soldiers?"

Dyer shook his head dispiritedly. "That's another blind alley. Fort Bliss hasn't any reports on any. But with all the men on furloughs and passes—and going through the city from other posts—it'll be weeks before we'll know for sure."

The door opened, and Captain Gerlach poked his head in. He said, "Hi, Mike," and then to the chief, "I've got a couple out here I'd like to have you talk to."

Dyer nodded. The captain opened the door and stepped back, saying, "Go right on in, folks. The chief will want to hear your story."

Shayne moved to go out as a middle-aged couple came in, but Gerlach stopped him. "You'd better sit in on this, too, Mike." He closed the door behind the couple and said, "This is Mr. and Mrs. Barton, Chief. They think they may have some information on the body we found in the river last night."

Mrs. Barton was a small lady with silvery hair. She had a sweet, unlined face, and she had been crying. The tears started flowing again as she took a step toward the chief's desk and said, "It's our boy. We know it is. The picture in the paper don't look like Jack but we know it's him."

Her husband was a tall, stooped man wearing what was evidently his "good" suit of blue serge, shiny in the seat and elbows, but neatly pressed. He moved to his wife's side and took her arm and said, "Now, Mother. We don't know for sure. Don't take on like that."

Captain Gerlach pushed a couple of chairs around for them, and Chief Dyer reseated himself. Mr. Barton got a clean white handkerchief from his pocket and pressed it into her withered hand, murmuring something in her ear.

She put the handkerchief up to her face and sobbed into it. Dyer asked, "Is your son missing?"

"Yes, sir. Jack's been gone since last Tuesday. We've tried not to worry, but when we read about it in the paper and how it said he wasn't identified yet, and all —well, we're afraid it's him."

"Does the description fit him?"

"It fits him too good," Mr. Barton said fearfully. "If we could look at him, sir. You haven't identified him yet, I reckon?" He leaned forward, despair overcoming the faint hope in his voice.

"Murder," Mrs. Barton sobbed through the handkerchief. "Jack said 'twould be murder, and that's what it is. If we'd only opened his letter in time to stop him—"

"Now, Mother." Mr. Barton clumsily patted his wife's shoulder. "No need to blame yourself. We couldn't stop him from going to see Mr. Towne. You know we couldn't. Jack was always that stubborn."

Captain Gerlach moved uneasily, and Chief Dyer's hand trembled as he took the cigarette holder away from his mouth. "Jefferson Towne?"

"Yes, sir. The big mining man. Him that's running for mayor. I dunno what this is in the paper about him killing a soldier last Tuesday, but I guess we better tell you the whole thing."

"I think you'd better," Dyer said dryly.

Mr. Barton reached inside his coat pocket and drew out a much-thumbed sheet of paper. He passed it across to Dyer, exclaiming dully, "Here's a letter Jack wrote last Tuesday just before he went out right after

noon. He left it pinned on his pillow and Mother
didn't find it till late that evening. But we didn't worry
so much after we read it, because a Mexican came by
about five o'clock to get Jack's Gladstone bag and he
said Jack was going on a trip and for us not to worry.
Jack had packed his bag, seems like, before he went
out, but he never said anything to us about it. You
better read the letter, and then you'll see why we think
it's Jack."

Dyer looked at Gerlach and Shayne as he unfolded
the sheet of paper. He mashed out his cigarette and
began to read aloud:

*Dear Mother and Dad—I can't stand the way things
are going any longer. I'm just a burden on you and
I'm going to quit letting you support me. You'll think
what I'm going to do is blackmail, but I don't care
any more. I'm leaving this note so you'll know who's
to blame if anything happens to me. I'm going to
see Mr. Jefferson Towne this afternoon and he has
promised to give me ten thousand dollars in cash to
pay me for keeping still about something I know so
he can win the election. But I don't trust Mr. Towne
and am afraid he may try to kill me to keep from
paying the money.*

*I'm going to take the risk because I don't see any
other way to quit being a burden on you. If I'm not
back by tonight when you find this, you'll know I'm
probably dead and Mr. Towne is responsible.*

*If that happens, take this letter to the police, and
get the notebook out of my Gladstone and take it to*

Mr. Neil Cochrane on the Free Press and he will give you $500 for the notebook, and he will use the information in it against Mr. Towne. I have sort of told Mr. Cochrane what it is and he has promised to pay that much for it. He suspects Mr. Towne will kill me instead of paying the money, and I'm leaving this letter at his suggestion.

No matter what happens I love you even if I haven't been much good. Jack.

Chief Dyer refolded the letter and laid it on his desk. Mrs. Barton's sobbing had ceased. She twisted the white handkerchief in her fingers and said falteringly, "You can see why we're so worried about Jack. We even got to wondering last night—when we read in the *Free Press* Extra about Mr. Towne being arrested— well, we got wondering if *that* had anything to do with Jack. It being on Tuesday afternoon and all."

"But Riley claims he saw Mr. Towne kill a soldier that afternoon."

"That's just it," she hurried on. "Jack was wearing khaki breeches and high laced boots and a tan shirt when he left home. Sort of like a soldier's uniform. Same color and all."

Dyer nodded thoughtfully. "But you hadn't worried about your son until then?"

"We worried about him plenty," Mr. Barton put in. "About what he'd gone and done. But we didn't think no harm had come to him, what with the Mexican coming for his Gladstone and saying he was going away on a trip. We thought, well, that he was ashamed to come back home after doing it and that he'd be writing to us."

"He was a good boy," Mrs. Barton cried out suddenly. "He never did anything bad in his life. He brooded about his sickness that kept him out of the army and a war job, and he worried about us not having much money."

"He's been changed and strange-acting since about a month ago when he came back from a prospecting trip in the Big Bend," Mr. Barton explained apologetically. "You see, he went to the School of Mines two years and then the doctors told him he should get out in the open, so he went off on a prospecting trip by himself and was gone almost six months. He came back different and bitter, sort of. Kind of blaming God, it seemed like, because a rich man like Mr. Towne had a big silver mine down there and he couldn't find nothing at all."

"He was downright blasphemous about the injustice of it," Mrs. Barton sobbed. "And we brought him up a good, religious boy, too."

"Then he tried to get a job out to Mr. Towne's smelter," Mr. Barton went on, "but they said he wasn't strong enough to do the work and he brooded over that some more. Then a couple of weeks ago he ups and goes off on a trip without saying nothing to us, and when he come back last Sunday he was extra cheerful and talked like he'd made some kind of strike. He never mentioned the bad thing he was planning to do when he left home Tuesday."

"Could we see him now?" Mrs. Barton pleaded.

"Seems like I can't go on wondering anymore. It'd be a blessed relief to just know it was him."

Dyer glanced at Gerlach. The homicide captain shook his head and explained, "They're busy fixing him up right now. Doc Thompson didn't get through with him until a little while ago, and they're fixing him to look as natural as possible. You'd better wait until this afternoon," he advised the Bartons in a kindly voice.

"Well, then, maybe we'd better go, Mother." Mr. Barton got up. She put the handkerchief to her face and began to sob again as she got up. He took her arm and tenderly guided her from the office. Gerlach went out with them and returned a few moments later. He shook his head angrily and asked, "Why do homicide victims invariably have parents like that?"

"How does it strike you?" Dyer asked.

He shrugged and admitted, "It seems to fit slick as a whistle. I never was satisfied with Riley's identification of the soldier's picture as Towne's victim, but I had an idea all the time he'd seen *something* down by the river Tuesday afternoon."

"Strike you that way, Shayne?" Dyer asked him.

"It makes sense," Shayne agreed. "Too much, maybe. Almost as though it was planned to fit."

"Do you mean to say you doubt their story—and this letter?" The chief struck the folded sheet of paper in front of him with his fist.

"I think they're straight enough all right." Shayne hesitated. "But I hardly see Towne playing the role it puts him in. Wouldn't young Barton warn him that such an incriminating letter existed? Towne would know he'd be arrested as soon as the body was fished from the river and identified."

'That's why he stripped all his clothes off. Hoping the body wouldn't be discovered until too late for it to be recognized as Jack Barton."

Shayne shook his head. "Jeff Towne hasn't gotten where he is by taking long chances. Let's not forget that Cochrane figures in this deal. He knew Jack Barton was going to meet Towne Tuesday afternoon to blackmail him. He'd already offered Barton five hundred for the information worth ten grand to Towne. It was Cochrane who warned Barton that Towne might kill him instead of paying off, and he advised the boy to leave an accusing letter behind."

"Isn't it what Cochrane would do?" Dyer demanded.

"Maybe. The question is, who got the Gladstone bag with the notebook containing the information? Someone sent a messenger to Barton's house for it."

"A Mexican messenger," Dyer stressed. "All Towne's servants are Mexicans. He sent for the bag, of course, after he'd put the boy out of the way."

"It looks that way," Shayne agreed. "Still, I'd like to hear what Cochrane knows. I'm interested to know what information Jack Barton had dug up against Towne."

"I think he's in the press room right now," Gerlach offered. "Shall I bring him in, Chief?"

Dyer said, "Sure," and fitted another cigarette into the end of his holder. Gerlach went out, and returned a few minutes later with Neil Cochrane. The reporter strutted in ahead of him with a thin smile of triumph on his lips. "Got a confession from Towne yet? Looks to me like we've got him dead to rights and—"

"We've just been talking to Mr. and Mrs. Barton," Dyer interrupted him.

The reporter stopped and tilted his head inquiringly. "Who?"

"Mr. and Mrs. Barton."

Cochrane blinked his eyes and looked doubtful. "Is that supposed to mean anything to me?"

Dyer said, "Sit down." He waited until Cochrane was seated before telling him, "Jack Barton's parents."

Cochrane pursed his lips and let out a thin whistle. He nodded wisely. "The lad who was carrying a grudge against Towne?"

"What was he blackmailing him with?"

Cochrane managed to look confused. "Who was blackmailing whom?"

"You were in on it," Dyer reminded him. "You offered the kid five hundred for his information if Towne didn't pay off."

Cochrane's eyes were very bright. He hunched his shoulder blades up and ducked his head forward. "All right. I haven't anything to hide. Sure, I offered him five C's for some dope that would fry Towne at the polls. Why not? The *Free Press* is always willing to pay for information in the public interest."

"What was that information?" barked Dyer.

"I don't know. He wouldn't tell me that. And I guess Towne paid off, all right," Cochrane added regretfully. "Young Barton was to see me Tuesday evening if there was any slip-up. I didn't see him."

"So he didn't tell you what it was?" Dyer snorted. "You went out on a limb and were willing to pay five hundred for information without knowing what it was?"

"Hell, no," Cochrane protested in an injured tone. "I told him it would be worth five hundred to my paper if it proved to be as hot as he claimed. He wouldn't even hint what it was. Only that it was plenty big enough to blast Towne out of the mayoralty race."

"Have you seen the body we pulled out of the river last night?" Gerlach demanded.

Cochrane twisted his neck to look at him, shaking his head slightly. "There was a picture of him in the morning paper but I didn't look at it closely."

"Remind you of anyone?" Dyer pounded at him.

"Why, no. I can't say that it—" Neil Cochrane clamped his lips together suddenly. A queer expression flitted across his face. He said, "By God," softly, and nodded. "Could be. Maybe I was right, huh, when I warned Barton he was playing with dynamite trying to blackmail Towne? Is *that* why he didn't get in touch with me?"

"So you do recognize the picture now?"

"Wait a minute," Cochrane protested warily. "I'm not saying I do. Hell, I only saw Barton twice. Same build, though. Same general features. And it adds up," he added eagerly. "The payoff was set for Tuesday afternoon. Same time Riley saw Towne choking a man by the river."

"A soldier," Dyer reminded him ironically. "Identified by Riley as Private James Brown by your own picture in the *Free Press*. Are you suggesting he choked two men by the river Tuesday afternoon?"

"No. But here's something to chew on. Both times I saw Barton, he was wearing khaki riding breeches and leather boots and a tan shirt. Not too much unlike a soldier's uniform. Do you suppose Riley could be mistaken in his identification, and actually saw Towne getting rid of a blackmailer?"

"Let's ask Towne," Dyer growled. He nodded curtly to Captain Gerlach and said, "Have him brought in."

CHAPTER FIFTEEN

Neil Cochrane sidled back into a corner of the room, pulling a chair with him as the captain went out. There was a smirk of satisfaction on his face as he settled down to wait for Towne to be brought in. Dyer scowled at him and warned, "You're not in the clear, Cochrane. Accessory to an extortion plot fits you like a glove."

Cochrane laughed shortly. "Accessory, hell! I did my best to talk the lad out of it. I warned him that Jeff Towne wasn't the sort to pay off without a fight."

"And you would much rather have had the information in print in the *Free Press* than see it suppressed," Shayne put in.

Cochrane grinned at him cockily. "I won't deny that. I tried to convince Jack Barton he'd be better off with my five hundred alive than trying to stick Towne for ten grand."

"But you didn't report it to us," Dyer pointed out. "You knew about the blackmail plot before Barton went to Towne. You took an active part in it by concealing guilty knowledge. I can lock you up for that."

"Perhaps," Cochrane conceded indifferently. "I won't stay locked up long if you do. And if you're smart, Chief, you'll start climbing on the bandwagon. Carter's going to be our next mayor and you know it as well as I do." He stretched out his thin shanks and yawned placidly.

Dyer clamped his teeth together, and his face reddened with impotent rage. He didn't look at Shayne. He sat behind his desk in glum silence until the door opened again and Gerlach ushered the prisoner in.

A night in jail had not improved Jefferson Towne's disposition, nor his appearance. There was a surly scowl on his rugged face, and his eyes were red-rimmed from worry and lack of sleep. His beard had sprouted raggedly during the night, and his clothing was rumpled.

He glared balefully at Shayne and Dyer as he strode into the room, demanded acidly, "Where's my attorney? Hasn't he showed up yet? What about a habeas corpus, or whatever it is? By God, I pay him an annual retainer—"

Dyer said, "Sit down, Towne, and tell us when you last saw Jack Barton."

Towne's expression did not change. He snorted, "Who's Jack Barton? How do I know when I saw him last? I want to phone Lionel Jackson. I'll tell him—"

"Right now you'd better tell *me* some things." Dyer's voice was uncompromising. "Sit down and relax. Mr. Jackson was in to see me early this morning trying to earn the retainer you pay his firm, but he didn't get very far."

"Riley's accusation is crazy on the face of it," Towne grated, dropping into a chair facing Dyer. "Anyone with the sense of a half-wit knows the soldier could have been dead only a few minutes before he was placed in the path of my car. Don't you think *I* would have known it, or the ambulance attendant, if he'd been dead for hours, as Riley claims?"

"That's been bothering us," Dyer admitted. "But I think we've found the answer to that now. We don't think you killed the soldier, Towne."

"So you've come to your senses at last." Towne started to rise.

Dyer said, "Sit down," and his voice cracked like a whiplash on a frosty morning. "You see, we know who you *did* kill down by the river a couple of hours before sundown."

Jefferson Towne sank back into his chair slowly. He looked bewildered but unworried. "I don't know what you're talking about."

"I think you do." Dyer tapped the folded letter on his desk. "Jack Barton left a letter explaining everything when he went out to meet you Tuesday. You see, he didn't quite trust you—thanks to Cochrane's suspicious mind," he added with a glance at the reporter in the corner.

Towne slowly turned his head to look in that direction. It was the first time he had seen Cochrane since he entered the office. "So you're in on this," he snarled. "I might have known you would be."

"I'm always happy to be of assistance to the authorities," Cochrane said blandly.

Towne turned back to Dyer. "What's this all about?"

"Jack Barton," Dyer reminded him. "What information was Barton holding over, you, Towne?"

"I don't know what you're talking about," Towne answered with tight-lipped precision.

Dyer sighed. "We've got it all down here." He tapped the folded letter again. "Didn't he warn you this was where it would be found if anything happened to him?"

Towne swore in a low monotone, said, "The double-crossing fool. Sure, he told me about the letter he'd left at home, and that his dope would go to the *Free Press* if I didn't pay off. But he wrote his folks a note telling them to tear the letter up and forget it. I dictated the note myself. He put a thousand dollars in it and mailed it before he caught the bus."

"You admit he was blackmailing you?"

"Sure, I admit it. I've known ever since yesterday afternoon that I'd probably have to tell the truth to clear myself. As soon as I heard Riley's accusation. I didn't think for a moment he actually believed it was the soldier he saw with me at the river. He made that story up to fit the printed facts," Towne ended in a tired voice.

"Whether he was fooled by Barton's khaki clothing or thought it really was a soldier is beside the point," Dyer said impatiently. "You admit you killed Barton rather than pay blackmail?"

"I admit nothing of the sort!" Towne shouted violently. "I had to knock him down and choke some sense into him. That's all. The damned fool expected me to pay out a cool ten thousand for nothing but his promise to keep quiet. I don't do business that way. I convinced him of that and we came to an understanding."

"Why didn't you tell us this last night?"

"Admit I was being blackmailed?" Towne asked. "I hoped the story wouldn't have to come out. I knew I couldn't be convicted of killing the soldier on that flimsy evidence. The timing was all wrong. I figured you'd have to apologize and release me after it was all over. I paid ten thousand dollars to keep this other thing quiet," he ended angrily.

"This understanding you claim you reached with young Barton. What was it?"

"Simple enough. I wouldn't give him the money until he turned the evidence over to me. And then he was to get out of town, and stay out until the election was over. And send his folks a note with a thousand in cash, telling them he was leaving and for them to tear up the letter he said he'd left behind. The one on your desk, I presume."

"Did he turn the stuff over to you?"

"I sent one of my men to his house to pick up his bag. I paid him the money after the notebook was in my hands. I dictated the note to his parents and he mailed it with ten hundred dollar bills just before he got on his bus for San Francisco."

"Did you see him get on that bus?"

"I certainly did. That was part of the agreement."

"How do you account for his body being fished out of the Rio Grande below El Paso last night?"

Jefferson Towne said, "Ridiculous."

"But true," said Dyer.

"I tell you I saw him get on the bus Tuesday evening."

"What time did the bus leave?"

"A little before six o'clock." Towne's head was lowered. He shook it like a mad bull ready to charge and bellowed, "There's some terrible mistake."

Chief Dyer's bald face was placid. He said, "His parents were here a little while ago to look at the body and they brought along this letter incriminating you. They didn't mention any note from their boy, nor any thousand dollars."

"They're playing some sort of game," Towne raged. "They read Riley's story and then about the finding of a body in the river and figured some sort of swindle."

"Do you know the Bartons?"

"Certainly not."

"It isn't any swindle," Dyer said. "They haven't heard from their boy since he left home to meet you around noon Tuesday."

Towne's rugged face looked harried. "I don't understand it," he muttered. "I saw him address the envelope. I saw him go to the mailbox and put it in. Do you suppose I would have let him get on the bus otherwise?" He jerked his head and challenged Dyer.

Dyer said mildly, "I don't think he did get on the bus."

"But I tell you—"

"Then how did his body get in the Rio Grande?"

"That's a mistake," Towne stated emphatically. "They lie if they identify the body as Jack Barton. I demand that you check up. Get another identification. I read this morning's paper and saw the picture of that drowned man. There might be a superficial resemblance to Jack Barton, but certainly no more than that."

Shayne was punishing his left earlobe and morosely gazing at the bare, dirty floor. He looked up abruptly and started to say something, but Chief Dyer said curtly, "That's all, Towne. We'll see to getting a positive identification." He nodded to Gerlach.

Gerlach stopped Towne's protestations by tapping him on the shoulder and taking a firm hold on his arm. Towne jerked his arm away and strode from the office.

Dyer asked Shayne, "What do you think of it now?"

"I'd like to know what Neil Cochrane was doing Tuesday afternoon," Shayne answered.

Cochrane emerged from his unobtrusive position, his face highly flushed. "Don't try to hang anything on me, shamus," he said.

"You were in on the blackmail deal," Shayne reminded him. "You hated to see that information against Towne slip out of your fingers. You were out of luck if Towne made the payoff as he claims, unless you could arrange some way to prevent that letter from reaching the Bartons—forcing them to make Jack's letter public."

"I can prove where I was Tuesday afternoon."

"You may have to." Shayne turned to Dyer and clamped his thumb and forefinger over his nose. "Don't you notice a stink in here Chief?"

Dyer said, "Get out, Cochrane."

Gerlach returned as the reporter went out. He sighed and said, "We seem to be going backward. Towne's story sounds straight."

"We'll bust it wide open after the parents identify the body this afternoon," Dyer predicted with confidence.

Shayne frowned heavily and said, "I wouldn't count on that too much, Chief."

"Why not? It must be the body of Jack Barton. Everything points to it."

"Everything," said Shayne softly, "except for the fact that the body was stripped naked."

"To make identification difficult. Hell, Shayne— Gerlach says it was you who first suggested that reason —when we still thought it might be a soldier."

"There's one thing wrong with that theory now. Jack Barton wasn't wearing army issue underwear and socks." Shayne stood up and rammed his hat down on his bristly red hair. "I'd get out a pick-up on Jack Barton, just on a chance. And I'd check the buses leaving Tuesday afternoon—to Frisco and any other points. And I'd like to know whether Towne drew ten thousand dollars out of his bank Tuesday."

"Naturally, we'll do all that," Dyer agreed. "You can't teach us routine police stuff, Shayne. You're the guy who's supposed to pull rabbits out of the hat."

"Maybe I'll do that, too." Shayne hesitated, then asked, "What do you know about Towne's silver mine in the Big Bend?"

"The Lone Star mine," Gerlach supplied. "Only big producer in all that region. Other small deposits have been found, but they always petered out."

"Near the border?"

"Not too far, I guess. The Southern Pacific has a spur track that takes off from somewhere below Van Horn."

"That wouldn't be too far from the old army camp at Marfa," Shayne mused.

"In that general neighborhood," Gerlach agreed.

"Do they still have trouble in the Big Bend? Mexican bandits and so on?"

Gerlach and Dyer both shook their heads. "Not for a good many years. They pulled the cavalry off the border years ago."

"But they still have a camp at Marfa, don't they?" Shayne persisted.

"Sure, but— Look here!" Dyer exploded, "What are you getting at now?"

Shayne said, "I wonder if Towne has any army guards from Marfa assigned to protect his mine or ore shipments—and if any of them are missing. I'm still looking for a logical explanation of that naked body." He turned and went out abruptly.

CHAPTER SIXTEEN

Behind the wheel of the police department automobile, it took Shayne a few minutes less than two hours to reach Van Horn. He pulled up at a filling station to inquire about the distance to Marfa and the road leading to Jefferson Towne's Lone Star silver mine.

The attendant told him it was about seventy miles to Marfa, and that the mine lay about fifty miles south of the main highway, with a road branching off to it a few miles out of Van Horn. There was another road direct to the mine from Marfa, he told the detective, making the two sides of the triangle only about a hundred miles if he wished to go to Marfa first and return via the mine.

Shayne thanked him and pulled out on the seventy-mile stretch through the greasewood and tabosa grass flats lying north of the mountainous Big Bend. It was a desolate road, with long tangents and sweeping curves, and Shayne settled back to make it as fast as he could. He had an idea it was going to prove a wasted effort, but there was no use passing up any bets while he was so close to the army camp. It would have been difficult for him to explain exactly why he was making this long trip. It was more a hunch than anything else. A hunch that wouldn't let him alone.

Somehow, mining and the Big Bend and soldiers

kept popping up in the case—or cases. There was the
young soldier who had been a miner in Mexico and
who was induced to enter the army under an alias
by some unknown person in El Paso, and there was
a second corpse stripped of his clothing in a manner
to indicate he might have worn a uniform before the
killing occurred. There was Josiah Riley who had been
fired and blackballed from the mining business by Jefferson Towne ten years ago, and there was young Jack
Barton, an unsuccessful mining engineer who had been
"changed," his father said, after a prospecting trip into
the Big Bend. After another brief disappearance from
home he had returned with some information about
Towne worth ten thousand to the mining magnate.

Somehow, they all tied together. Along with, Shayne
told himself morosely, Lance Bayliss, who had been a
Nazi sympathizer; a racketeer and former smuggler
named Manny Holden; a Mexican girl who had a yen
for American soldiers on the wrong side of the Rio
Grande, and was also the daughter of Towne's Mexican
paramour; and an Austrian refugee named Larimer,
who ran a secondhand clothing store; plus Neil Cochrane, who had once loved Carmela Towne and now
hated both her and her father and, presumably, Lance
Bayliss, who had won her love while Neil was courting
her.

It all added up into a hell of a tangle. That was the
only thing he was positive about. But there had to be a
connecting link somewhere. There were soldiers in the
Big Bend, and there was a silver mine. The soldiers
were stationed there to protect American property

from the depredations of bandits from across the border.

Shayne didn't know whether that was important or not. He had a hazy idea that it might be.

He was glad when the little sun-baked cowtown of Marfa showed against the horizon ahead. The army post was in plain view on the flats south of town. Shayne turned off before reaching the business district, drove through the Mexican section out to the post.

A bored sentry stopped him at the entrance. Shayne showed his credentials and explained that he was co-operating with the El Paso police in clearing up the murder of an army man, and asked to speak to the commanding officer.

The sentry waved him on toward post headquarters and advised him to ask for Colonel Howard. Shayne parked in front of a one-story concrete building and went in. An orderly directed him along a corridor to the open door of a large, plainly furnished office. An erect, military figure sat behind a flat desk. He was broad-shouldered and middle-aged, with brown eyes and a clipped mustache.

He looked up from some papers and nodded pleasantly enough when Shayne walked in. The detective introduced himself and explained that he represented the civilian authorities in El Paso, who were investigating the death of one soldier and the possible death of another.

"A second body was found in the Rio Grande last night, stripped to the skin," Shayne explained. "He was murdered at approximately the same time the other soldier was killed, and in a somewhat similar manner. We think he may have been stripped to hide the fact that he was wearing a uniform and to deter identification."

Colonel Howard was interested. He knew of Michael Shayne by reputation, and had read press reports of the Private Brown case. He asked why Shayne had come to see him.

"To learn whether any of your men have been missing since last Tuesday—or before that."

The colonel shook his head and said he didn't think so, but he would have the matter checked. He called in a corporal and issued instructions. The corporal promised to have the report in a few minutes and disappeared into an inner office. "But why come to Marfa, Mr. Shayne?" Colonel Howard asked interestedly. "There are many larger army posts nearer El Paso."

"I happened to be in this vicinity," Shayne explained, "and didn't want to pass up any bets." He paused to light a cigarette. "Do you still maintain any sort of border patrol? Have any squads or troops on detached duty along the Rio Grande?"

"Not as a regular thing. The old posts up and down the river at Candelaria, Ruidosa, Presidio, and so forth have been abandoned for many years. We send out patrols only in case of a raid or some unusual disturbance."

"Then—patrolling the border to prevent smuggling or illegal entry isn't part of your routine?" Shayne persisted.

The colonel told him it wasn't. "There are Customs

men at the Ports of Entry, of course, and Texas keeps a few rangers stationed in the Big Bend. But there hasn't been any serious trouble here for years."

Shayne's blunt fingertips drummed impatiently on the colonel's desk. "Any spy scares in this vicinity, or even a hint of subversive influences?"

The colonel laughed gently. "We're a small unit, completely isolated here, Mr. Shayne. I'm afraid a spy wouldn't learn much of value in Marfa."

The corporal returned to report that their records showed no men A.W.O.L.

Shayne thanked the colonel and started to get up. He asked casually, "Has Jefferson Towne ever requested troops to guard his mine ore shipments?"

"The Lone Star mine near the border? I haven't heard of any trouble there."

"Are any of your troops stationed near there—or is it on a main road traveled by your patrols?"

"No," the colonel answered. "The mine is located in a rough and isolated section of the mountains. So far as I know, none of my men have been near the mine."

Shayne thanked him for his help. He went out and drove back to Marfa, and headed southward into the mountains on a rough dirt road. The road became winding and dangerous as it climbed upward into the low mountains, and it was mid-afternoon when he came to a railroad crossing paralleled by a wider and smoother road. Two pointed pine boards were nailed to a tree. One pointed to the left and read LONE STAR MINE. The other pointed to the right and read VAN HORN 50 MI.

Turning to the left, he climbed steeply for a little more than a mile, stopping in front of high steel gates padlocked together with a heavy chain. When opened, the double gates were wide enough to accommodate both railroad track and the automobile driveway. A twelve-foot woven-wire fence led away from the gates in both directions, surmounted by three strands of barbed wire leaning outward at a forty-five degree angle. A sign on one of the gates read KEEP OUT.

Shayne cut off his motor and sat with his big red hands gripping the steering wheel. Through the steel gates he could see an unpainted shed about fifty feet beyond the gate. Farther up the slope were several low buildings that appeared to be bunkhouses and tool sheds. On the left was a huge loading bin on high stilts with the rails leading beneath in order that gondolas could be spotted there to receive their load of ore fed to the bin from the mine entrance by a gravity chute down the hillside.

The whole place was unaccountably deserted. He listened intently for some sound of miners at work, then realized that production was probably at a lower level and any sounds of activity would be muffled.

He got out of the car after a moment and sauntered toward the padlocked gates. A man came out of the nearby shed and looked at him. He wore a greasy black Stetson and corduroy pants, and the wide cartridge belt around his waist sagged with the weight of a bolstered six-shooter on his right hip. He took cigarette papers and a sack of Bull Durham from his shirt pocket and began to roll a cigarette. Shayne stopped in front of the gates and shouted, "Hey!" The guard licked his brown-paper cigarette and stuck it between his lips. He lit it and hooked his thumbs in his gun belt and strolled forward. "Whatcha want?"

"Unlock this damned gate so I can drive in."

"Gotta permit?"

"A what?" Shayne asked incredulously.

"A permit." The guard stopped on the other side of the gates, peering at him suspiciously.

Shayne said, "For God's sake! I'm not going to steal any of your damned silver ore."

"Ain't got no permit, huh?" The man shook his head disapprovingly.

"What kind of a permit?" Shayne demanded.

"One that's signed by Mr. Towne. That's what kind." The guard tugged the brim of his hat lower over his eyes and started to turn away.

"Wait a minute," Shayne said. "I'm a friend of Mr. Towne's. He sent me out here to look over some machinery."

"What machinery?"

"The hoisting engine," Shayne hazarded. "It's getting old and needs some repairs."

The man shook his head and spat contemptuously. "That won't work, Mister. Not without you gotta permit signed with Mr. Towne's name."

"What in the name of God is all the secrecy about?"

The man shrugged. "Guv'ment orders," he said vaguely. "Silver's a mighty important war material an' we're clost to the border here. Them're my orders, anyhow, an' no amount of fast talkin' won't get you in."

Shayne said, "Mr. Towne will fire you when he hears about this."

The man spat again and then walked back toward his shack. Shayne stared after him impotently. The man went inside, and that seemed to be an end to it.

Shayne went back and wheeled his coupé around and sped back toward El Paso.

CHAPTER SEVENTEEN

It was less than a three-hour drive back from the mine. Shayne drove straight to police headquarters and went in. He found Chief Dyer with his hat on ready to go out to eat. The chief looked tired and disgusted. He grunted, "Where've you been hiding all afternoon?"

"Around and about." Shayne eyed him speculatively. "Things been happening?"

Dyer nodded. He took off his hat and looked at it as if surprised to find it on his head. He threw it down on his desk and said, "Plenty."

"Have you got time to bring me up to date?"

Chief Dyer sighed and sat down in his swivel chair. "I haven't any place to go," he confessed. "I just wanted to get away from this damned office before a couple of gremlins sneak in to inform me that there haven't been any murders or dead bodies or any other damned thing."

"Is it that bad?" asked Shayne.

"Just about. The whole thing's blown up. We're all the way out on a limb, and I'm wailing for it to be sawed off."

Shayne draped himself on a chair and said, "Give."

"First thing is the Bartons. They came down about two o'clock with a note they'd just received in the mail from their son. It was postmarked last Tuesday. Mailed in a downtown box."

"With ten one-hundred-dollar bills?"

"That's right. Just like Towne said."

"What the hell has it been doing in the mail ever since Tuesday?"

"One of those things," Dyer groaned, "that walk up and slap us in the face sometimes. I don't live right, Shayne. That's all there is to it. What happens to me shouldn't happen to a dog."

Shayne said, "I'm listening."

"The envelope was addressed wrong. In his hurry or excitement, Jack Barton neglected to put a 'South' in front of the street name. So it went out by the wrong carrier. Came back to the main post office, where they looked in the directory and found the Bartons lived on *South* Vine. So it didn't reach them until the afternoon delivery today."

"No doubt about its authenticity?"

"None at all," Dyer sighed. "They recognized their son's handwriting, and I had it checked by an expert with the other note he left. In it, he told them he was leaving town hurriedly and for them to tear up the other note he'd left behind without reading it. Exactly what Towne told us he dictated to him."

"I wondered about that," Shayne admitted. "It sounded like the sort of thing Towne *would* do. He couldn't afford to ship Jack Barton out of the city without taking some precaution to prevent the other letter from reaching us. He figured the grand would tie the old folks' hands—that, and the knowledge that their son was a blackmailer. It seems to me that arrival of the note clarifies things," he added encouragingly.

"You haven't heard half of it yet," Dyer growled. "I insisted that they look at the body anyway, with some crazy idea, I guess, that Cochrane had gotten mixed into it after Towne made the payoff."

"And the body isn't Jack Barton?" Shayne guessed easily.

"Definitely not. They're both absolutely positive. I watched their faces while they looked at it, and I'm convinced they were telling the truth."

Shayne shrugged. "It really couldn't have been Barton. It didn't make sense that way. Towne would know a body thrown in the river would have to show up eventually. If he killed Barton he certainly would have disposed of the body so it couldn't ever be identified again."

"I don't know about that," Dyer argued. "Getting rid of a corpse isn't that easy. Plenty of murderers have tried it and failed. All sorts of elaborate schemes. You know that."

"Sure, it's difficult," Shayne agreed. "But he could have devised something a lot better than just stripping the body and throwing it into the river. No, after I heard Towne's story this morning, I felt sure the naked body wasn't Jack Barton."

"Who is it, then?" Chief Dyer demanded hoarsely.

"If I knew that, I'd know the rest of the story. I suppose you checked the other angles Towne gave us this morning?"

"Sure. And they all proved out just like he said. He withdrew ten thousand dollars from his bank Tuesday in hundred-dollar bills. He specified old bills without consecutive serial numbers. A bus leaves for Frisco at six P.M. and the ticket seller vaguely remembers a man like Towne buying a ticket a short time before departure, and the driver remembers him hanging around until the bus pulled out. He couldn't positively identify a picture of Jack Barton as a passenger, but thinks he was probably aboard."

"Were you able to get anything more out of Towne on his reason for paying blackmail?"

"Not a damned thing. He insists that's his own business, and there's no law to compel him to tell." Chief Dyer spread out his hands morosely. "There you are. The whole damned thing blown up in our faces. Towne's in the clear. He admits having an altercation with the boy and beating him up some, but hell, we can't hang a charge on that."

"So you released him?"

"What else could we do? The Barton story blows Riley's accusation sky-high." Dyer's voice trembled with indignation. "Riley backed down completely when confronted with the facts. He admitted the man he saw Towne attack might have been dressed in khaki prospecting clothes instead of a uniform as he supposed, and that he wasn't actually close enough to positively identify any features. Damn witnesses who tell one story and then crawl out of it," he ended angrily.

Shayne settled back, lit a cigarette, and puffed thoughtfully. "No more dope on any other missing soldiers or any of those angles?"

"Not a single damned thing." Dyer thumped his desk with an exasperated fist. "We're right back where we started. I don't see that the body in the river has anything to do with the other thing."

"No identification yet?"

"None at all. We got a set of prints and sent them in to Washington after checking with our files. A thousand people have looked at him in the morgue this afternoon, and none of them ever saw him before. There is one thing, though," he added grudgingly.

Shayne tugged at his left earlobe and waited.

"It isn't much. Probably nothing. We've been tailing that Mexican girl, you know?"

"Marquita Morales?"

"Yes. And by the way, her mother seems to be a very decent sort. Thinks her daughter is a good girl going to school in Juarez. Doesn't suspect her extracurricular activities."

Shayne nodded gravely. "That doesn't surprise me."

"She made another pick-up this afternoon. Couple of young privates from Bliss with a three-day pass. She took them into a secondhand clothing store about an hour ago, and came out with two young fellows in civilian clothes."

"Larimer's shop?" Shayne asked sharply.

"No. Another one of the same type about two blocks away. My man had his instructions this time and didn't ball things up by pulling a pinch. We notified Army Intelligence and they put a watch on the shop."

"And the girl?"

"She went over to Juarez on a streetcar with her pick-ups."

"How do they get away with it?" Shayne demanded.

"Don't persons crossing the border have to produce some sort of identification in wartime?"

"Sure they do. And they had it. My man was on the car with them. The two soldiers had registration cards all in order. 4-Fs, both of them."

Shayne nodded slowly. His eyes were alight now. "It begins to look like a well-planned business. Renting civvies and fake identification cards to soldiers who want to cross the border."

"Looks like it," Dyer agreed unemotionally. "Not too much harm in that, though. The boys have to blow off steam somehow."

"If that's all it amounts to," Shayne agreed. "Is your tail still on Marquita and her two escorts?"

"That's out of our jurisdiction. But he did turn her over to a Mexican detective on the other side. They're keeping watch on her tonight—and on the two soldiers."

"The Juarez police sound more cooperative than they used to be," Shayne commented wryly.

"There's a new municipal set-up over there. They've helped us all they could."

Shayne asked, "How about putting me in touch with the right people on that side?"

"What for?"

"I've got a hankering to take a look at the seamier side of Juarez, and I imagine following Marquita around would be a good way to see it all."

Dyer studied him suspiciously for a moment, but Shayne's wide-mouthed grin gave no indication of the detective's real thoughts. He lifted his telephone and gave a Juarez number. He talked to a Captain Rodriquiz for a time, and then hung up and nodded to Shayne.

"They've got a man on her. See Captain Rodriquiz at headquarters and he'll arrange a contact. And I," he added violently, "am going to buy a bottle of aspirin and a quart of whisky and go home to bed."

Shayne's grin widened, and he warned him, "Don't hit either of them too hard. An inner voice tells me that things are ready to start popping again." He went out with a blithe wave of his hand.

CHAPTER EIGHTEEN

Captain Rodriquiz of the Juarez police force was a slim, elegantly clad young Mexican with flashing white teeth and a thin black mustache. He spoke impeccable English and looked intelligent. He greeted Shayne warmly at police headquarters, assured him it was an honor to be associated with the famous American detective on a case, and offered his services as a guide for the evening.

"That won't be necessary," Shayne demurred. "If you'll just put me in touch with the man who is tailing the girl and the two soldiers—"

"But I wish to accompany you," Rodriquiz insisted. "You think it is important—this girl and the soldiers?" He put on a small black hat with a tiny red feather in the band and led Shayne out of the police building.

"I don't know," Shayne admitted. "It's likely to be a blind alley, and I'm afraid you'll be bored."

"Please, Mr. Shayne. It will be a pleasure. We will walk, if you like. At present the girl and her escorts are at *El Gato Pobre*. It is but a short distance."

"I've eaten there," Shayne told him. "Best food in Juarez since the Mint closed. But it's hardly the place I'd expect Marquita to hang out unless it's changed a lot in ten years."

"Oh, no. It is the same. It is early, and they go there for dinner and drinks. Later, Marquita will take her soldiers to the other places."

"Still running wide open?"

Captain Rodriquiz shrugged elaborately, a broad smile exhibiting his white teeth. "It is what you Americans expect when you cross the border for a night out. We would be sorry to disappoint you by closing them."

"Marijuana and the pipe joints—and all the rest?" Shayne persisted.

"I think you will find in El Paso or any other American city the same," his guide protested somewhat stiffly. "In Juarez we do not turn our backs and pretend it is not so."

Shayne admitted the justice of the rejoinder. They strolled along the 16th of September Street to Juarez Avenue, turned to the right, and then off onto a side street and into *El Gato Pobre Café.*

There was a long bar just off the entrance, a check room at the left. Half a dozen prosperous-appearing Mexicans were drinking at the bar. Rodriquiz said, "I think we will have a drink," and wandered to the end of the bar. Shayne ordered a double shot of *aguardiente,* and the captain took *tequila* with a slice of lemon.

The bartender nodded to Rodriquiz while taking their orders, and lingered to wipe off the bar after setting the drinks before them. Rodriquiz murmured a few words of Mexican Spanish into his ear, and he nodded again. He went back through an inner door leading into the café, and was gone a couple of minutes. He went on serving drinks without another glance at the captain and Shayne after returning.

Shayne sipped his *aguardiente* and wished he had thought to order a chaser. An inconspicuous little man came out of the café and sidled up to Rodriquiz. He ordered a glass of beer and began talking in a low monotone.

After he finished his beer, he went out the front door.

"The girl and her soldiers are inside eating dinner," Rodriquiz told Shayne. "Do you think she would recognize you?"

Shayne said, "I don't think so. Not if we sat some distance from her." He finished his drink and added wryly, "I just remembered I've had neither lunch nor dinner."

"We will go inside," the Mexican officer decided. "There are tables in the corners behind palms where you can dine while we watch."

They went into a large dining room with less than half of the tables occupied. There was a small dance floor in the center with a string quartet on a platform. They were playing a Mexican melody, and half a dozen couples were dancing.

Rodriquiz led the way to a table in one corner near the door, partially screened from the rest of the room by two potted palms. When they were seated, he gestured toward the dance floor and said, "Is that not Marquita at the table near the platform?"

Shayne's gaze followed the gesture, and he nodded.

Marquita wore a black dress, cut low and square across the front with thin straps over her shoulders. She wore a lot of rouge and looked very vivacious and pretty at that distance. Her companions were young, and had evidently been drinking quite a lot. They both wore gray suits that didn't fit too well, and they laughed a lot, and both of them sat close to Marquita.

"They are eating dinner slowly, and we will have plenty of time," Rodriquiz assured Shayne when a waiter put menus in front of them. "You will excuse me, for I have eaten."

Shayne looked at the typewritten menu and ordered, "Roast mallard with chestnut dressing." He hesitated, and asked the captain, "Do I dare order an American cocktail?"

"It will be of the best quality," Rodriquiz told him.

Shayne told the waiter, "Two sidecars," and looked inquiringly at his companion. Rodriquiz smiled and said, "I will have *tequila* with lemon."

Marquita got up to dance with one of her soldiers. Her dress was as short as the skirt Shayne had seen her wearing previously. She pressed her body shamelessly against her dancing-partner and showed the rolled tops of her stockings and an expanse of tanned thighs as she whirled around the dance floor.

The dining room filled slowly as Shayne ate his dinner. He stiffened slightly when he saw the hunched shoulder blades and bushy head of Neil Cochrane come through the door. He moved his chair slightly so he was farther behind a palm frond when Cochrane stepped aside to wait by the door after a few words with the headwaiter.

Captain Rodriquiz alertly noted Shayne's glance and his movement to conceal himself from the waiting man. He lifted his black brows and asked politely, "Is it someone you would avoid?"

"He's an El Paso reporter," Shayne muttered. *"Could* be that he's here for the same reason I am."

At that instant Cochrane spotted Marquita returning to her table. He watched her for a moment, and then threaded his way toward her. He stopped at her table and leaned over the back of her chair to speak to her, and from across the room, Shayne and Rodriquiz could see that she was introducing him to her companions. He took the empty chair at their table, and one of the soldiers ordered another round of drinks.

Shayne settled back and shook his head. He admitted, "I don't know, Captain. It looks as though he planned to meet her here with those two lads. If that's it—" He shook his red head again and his eyes were worried. "Let's sit tight and see what happens."

A Mexican girl came out on the stage and sang *"Estrellita."* She had a beautiful, clear voice that hadn't been ruined by too much nightclub work, and she sang the song with artistry. She didn't get much applause when it was over, and she didn't stay for an encore. The quartet swung into *"Besame Mucho,"* and Neil Cochrane and Marquita got up to dance. She didn't press herself flagrantly against him as she had with the soldier, and he appeared to be an awkward dancer. They were discussing something as they moved about the dance floor, and neither of them seemed particularly happy. They went back to the table as soon as the one number was over.

Shayne was watching them, and didn't see Carmela Towne come in the door. He saw Cochrane straighten up after Marquita was seated, and glance toward the door. The reporter then said something to the trio and left them.

Shayne looked toward the door and saw Carmela standing just inside. She wore a belted sports outfit that was too young for her and accentuated her thinness. Her lips were heavily rouged, but her cheeks were pale. Her dark, deep-set eyes glittered and flashed from Cochrane, who was moving toward her, to Marquita and her two young escorts.

Cochrane smiled as he approached Carmela. Neither of them seemed surprised to see the other, indicating a pre-arranged meeting. He took her arm and drew her aside to a small table for two. Shayne stayed behind the palm and kept his face averted. He said to Rodriquiz, who was watching everything with alert interest, "We may have to separate. You take the Mexican girl and her two companions if they leave first. The woman who just met the reporter at the door is Miss Towne, daughter of Jefferson Towne. I want to keep them in sight."

Captain Rodriquiz said, "So?" He watched the couple intently. "They've ordered a drink and are talking," he reported. "She asks him questions and is not pleased when he shakes his head and refuses to reply."

"The others are paying their check," Shayne warned him. "You follow them out and I'll take care of the check here."

"There will be no check at this table," the captain said. "It will be, as you say, on the house."

The trio had left their table by the dance floor and were going out. Shayne kept his face averted, but Rodriquiz chuckled, "I think Miss Towne does not like Marquita. She gives what you call a dirty look as they pass."

He pushed his chair back and got up, went toward the door behind the three. Shayne lit a cigarette and smoked it, resting one side of his face against the open palm of one hand to shield it from Carmela and Neil Cochrane, occasionally peering cautiously at them.

He need not have taken that precaution. Neither of them was paying any attention to anyone else. They had ordered cocktails but were not drinking them. It was evident that Carmela was tensed to a high pitch. Her movements were jerky, and she puffed rapidly on a cigarette, exhaling the smoke immediately in quick puffs. They were having an unpleasant argument, and Cochrane was evidently enjoying it. There was a sly, sadistic smile on his vulturous face, and he kept shaking his head in response to Carmela's entreaties.

She got up suddenly, her body stiffly erect and her eyes blazing at Cochrane. He stood up, smiling insolently, pausing to get out a wallet, and let two bills flutter to the table beside their untasted drinks. Shayne hunched farther away from them and looked in the other direction. He waited a few minutes before going out. Carmela and Cochrane had disappeared, but he was surprised to see Captain Rodriquiz loitering in the outer doorway.

The captain smiled and beckoned to him when he hesitated. "It is all right," the captain assured him. "Your couple have just gone out. Marquita and her soldiers stopped at the bar for a drink and are only slightly ahead." He looked down the street and nodded "They are close together down there."

Shayne stepped out with him. Marquita and her escorts were just turning to the right onto Juarez Avenue, and Carmela and Cochrane were less than twenty feet behind them. When they also turned the corner to the right, Shayne started forward, muttering, "I wonder what in hell this is all about. Looks as though Miss Towne and Cochrane were following the others."

"I do not think so," Rodriquiz objected. "Unless they knew they would stop at the bar for a drink. They would be long out of sight, otherwise. Of course," he added politely, "I do not understand the connection between all of these."

"Neither do I," Shayne muttered. He held back as they reached the avenue. "You'd better take a look."

Rodriquiz sauntered past the corner. He shrugged, and paused to light a cigarette, taking some time with it. Then he nodded to Shayne. "It is all right, I think."

Carmela and Cochrane had lengthened their dis-

tance to almost a full block when Shayne rounded the
corner. The other three were still the same distance
ahead. Carmela's bare head with its smoothly coiled
braids of black hair was inches above Cochrane's. She
held herself proudly and moved with a swinging stride
that caused him to hurry his short legs to keep pace.

Shayne and the Mexican police captain loitered along
the full block behind, through a section of respectable
business houses, and on into the furtive darkness of
unlighted streets lined with heavily curtained houses
crowding close to the sidewalks. They moved closer
after leaving the lighted avenue behind, up to within
fifty feet of the rear pair. The others were still slightly
ahead, evidenced by Marquita's light giggle from time
to time, and answering laughter from her tipsy companions.

"I think Marquita will go first to Papa Tonto's," Rodriquiz whispered cautiously after they had traversed
three blocks in this manner. "We have the report that
she is seen there much. It is a bad place," he went on
in answer to Shayne's unspoken query. "If they turn
down the alley in the next street, we will know."

There were no streetlights at all now, and thin clouds
partially obscured the moon, but the trailing men were
close enough to hear the others moving steadily ahead.

There was a queer tightness in Shayne's chest and
his mouth was dry as he continued on doggedly. He
was thinking of Carmela Towne in her living room last
night—and, later, crumpled unconscious in her bed.
He should have stayed with her until the liquor wore

off. She had been in no condition to be left to awaken alone in that echoing stone house. He thought, *God knows how she must have felt when she woke up and found me gone.*

And tonight she was walking down a squalid street in Juarez by the side of Neil Cochrane whom she detested. *Why?* Where was she going? What was the meaning of this secret meeting with Cochrane?

There was a sudden break in the clouds overhead, and a bleary moon shone down on the street briefly, outlining Carmela's bare head and squared shoulders and the shambling figure of Neil Cochrane by her side as they approached the alley entrance. Ahead of them, the street was empty. Rodriquiz nodded wisely and murmured, "It is as I thought. They have turned in the alley to Papa Tonto's."

Even as he spoke, the pair ahead of them turned into the alley also. At the same time, the clouds came together again, hiding the moon behind a heavier veil than before. Far off toward the river a burro brayed dismally, and Shayne shuddered in spite of himself. He gripped Rodriquiz's arm and urged him forward roughly, muttering, "I don't like this. Let's hurry—"

The muffled *brup* of a small-caliber pistol from the darkness of the alley interrupted him. A single scream followed the shot, then two more sharp, blasting reports in quick succession. Shayne was lunging into the alley, and Rodriquiz panted by his side.

They halted beside a blurred shape in the alley, and Shayne dropped to his knees and put his arms about

Carmela's shaking shoulders. She was crouched, sobbing, over the lifeless body of Neil Cochrane, and her
face was a blurred oval of whiteness in the dark when
she lifted it to look at him. "Michael?" she sobbed.
"Hurry! You've got to find Lance. In that place! Papa
Tonto's." She sank back in his arms limply.

CHAPTER NINETEEN

Captain Rodriquiz was squatting beside them and he twitched a stubby pistol from Carmela's fingers before she dropped it. He said swiftly to Shayne, "I will stay here if you wish. Papa Tonto's is where the light shines at the end of the alley."

"The killer ran that way, too," Carmela moaned. "I shot at him but I don't think—I hit him."

Shayne let her lax body down on the ground and stood up. Inhabitants of the neighborhood, aroused by the three shots, were beginning to stream toward them. Shayne muttered, "I'll take a look in Tonto's—for the other three who were ahead, and for Lance."

He trotted down the alley to a closed wooden door with a dim light bulb glowing above it. The door was unlocked, and he strode into a dark hallway. Light showed through curtains at the other end of the hall.

An old Mexican came out of an alcove to confront him as he started forward. He had thin white hair, and luminous eyes set in a wrinkled face. He laid a palsied hand on Shayne's arm and protested, "No, Señor. I am not know you, an' you cannot—"

Shayne thrust him off with a force that sent him reeling back against the wall. He went on to the curtains and thrust them aside. The low room was lighted with a few bulbs in the ceiling, partially obscured by a heavy pall of smoke hanging above the couples who sat at small tables or half reclined in booths about the wall. The smoke was acrid and biting in his nostrils, heavy with the noxious fumes of marijuana. The couples were young and mostly Mexican. They looked up at him vacantly as he threaded his way between the tables, and those in the booths didn't change their amorous attitudes as he paused to peer in at each couple. Neither Marquita Morales and her escorts nor Lance Bayliss was in the room.

The old man from the entrance panted up to him when he finished his inspection at the far end of the room. *"Qué busca usted?"* he demanded.

"I'm looking for a girl and two Americans who just came in," Shayne growled. "Any other places where people hide out in here?"

"But no, *Señor.*" His voice trembled angrily. *"Nadie se esconde."*

Shayne snorted, and jerked aside another curtain over the entrance to a short corridor leading off from the main room. The odor of opium swept out strongly. Four doors opened off the corridor into small cubicles fitted with beds and smoking equipment. Two of the cubicles were empty. A middle-aged American woman lay on her back in another bed. Her mouth was open and she was snoring. The small room was stifling with opium smoke. Shayne closed the door hastily after one look at her. The fourth cubicle had two occupants, and two pipes were going strongly. They were young, a Mexican and an American girl. They didn't pay any attention to Shayne when he looked in on them. They were off in a dream world of their own.

The corridor dead-ended, and there was no other exit. Shayne stalked back through the main room and out through the curtains into the dark entrance hallway. The old Mexican's eyes blazed at him balefully from the alcove as he went by, but he didn't speak.

In the alley an ambulance and a police car were drawn up at the entrance, with their lights shining on a group of people near the end. Neil Cochrane's body was being loaded into the ambulance. Carmela hurried toward Shayne, with Rodriquiz a few paces behind. Carmela's face was white and her smoothly braided hair was disarranged. Her eyes burned into his as she caught his arm and cried frantically, "Where is he, Michael? Did you find him? Was Lance there?"

Shayne shook his head. He put his arm about her shoulders and told the Mexican police captain, "Marquita and her friends evidently didn't go into Tonto's. What have you done out here?"

"We will find them," Rodriquiz assured him confidently. The pistol he had taken from Carmela still dangled from his fingers. He glanced down at it and suggested politely, "If you will ride in the car with me?"

Carmela leaned against Shayne with her face pressed to his chest. "I don't understand, Michael. Where's Lance? I don't—" She began to sob violently.

Shayne nodded to Rodriquiz and picked her up in his arms. He carried her to the police car and got in the back seat with her. Captain Rodriquiz got in the front beside a uniformed driver. The ambulance was already backing away. Rodriquiz turned to tell Shayne, "We have blocked off this section and are searching for Marquita and her two soldiers. The man you looked for in Papa Tonto's—?"

Shayne shook his head. Carmela sat beside him, supported by his arm about her, with her head resting against his shoulder. She said tiredly, like a small child just awakened from deep sleep, "They told me Lance was there. I don't know—"

Shayne said, "We'll talk about it when we get to headquarters." He tightened his arm about her, and she sighed and didn't say anything else.

At the police station, Captain Rodriquiz escorted them back to a private office. He seated himself gravely at a desk and had a stenographer brought in, laying Carmela's pistol in front of him. She sat beside Shayne and held his hand tightly. Before the captain could begin asking questions, Shayne asked him, "What about the man who was killed, Captain?"

"Quite dead." Rodriquiz raised his expressive eyebrows. "One bullet fired against his body penetrated the heart." He looked at Carmela. "Will you tell us, please, how it happened?"

"Wait a minute," Shayne said. "She should be told anything she says may be used against her. And you can consult an attorney first," he told Carmela, "or refuse to testify at all, if you wish."

"Oh, no," she said quickly. "I want to tell you everything. Why should I refuse?"

Shayne shrugged. "Go ahead then."

"There isn't much to tell." She paused to moisten

her lips. "We had just turned into the alley, and it was awfully dark. Neil was a step ahead of me—and the first thing I heard was the gun going off. Neil groaned and fell before I realized what had happened. Then I heard someone running. I couldn't actually see in the darkness, but I realized he'd been shot and his murderer was getting away. I instinctively got my pistol out of my bag and fired after him. I shot twice. And then I heard someone running up behind me. I didn't know it was you, Michael." She rubbed her eyes as though still bewildered. "I didn't know you were anywhere in Juarez. And—that's all," she ended simply.

Rodriquiz looked at Shayne and shrugged. He asked Carmela, "You will swear the pistol was in your handbag when the first shot was fired?"

"Oh, yes. It was."

"And you fired only two shots, *after* Mr. Cochrane had fallen and his assailant was running away?"

"That's right. That's the way it happened."

Captain Rodriquiz opened the small revolver and drew out three empty brass cylinders, which he carefully lined up in front of him. The gun was a .38 with its barrel sawed off half an inch from the cylinder to make it a small though lethal weapon.

"There is one empty chamber," he pointed out to Shayne and Carmela. "Behind that there are three empty cartridges. Then two loaded ones." He drew out the two unexploded .38 shells. They had snub-nosed, leaden heads, and two deep notches in the shape of a cross were cut in the soft nose of each bullet. He lined the two bullets up with the empty cylinders and said, "Your pistol has been fired three times, Miss Towne."

"Perhaps I shot three times. I don't know. I don't remember." Carmela shuddered violently. "I *thought* I just pulled the trigger twice."

Shayne leaned over to pick up one of the bullets, and he studied it with a frown. "Homemade dum-dums," he muttered. "Who taught you to fix bullets this way, Carmela?"

"Father fixed them for me. Years ago when he gave me that gun. He said"—her voice faltered and then came clearly—"they were more deadly that way. And that I should never use it until I had to, but if it ever came to a showdown, that I should shoot to kill."

"And tonight was the first time you had to use it?" murmured Rodriquiz.

"Yes, I—I haven't carried that pistol, or even thought about it, for years, until tonight." She glanced from the Mexican captain to Shayne. "Why are you both looking like that?"

Shayne shrugged, and reached over to replace the bullet. "There were only three shots filed in the alley, Carmela. Rodriquiz and I were right behind you. One of the three bullets killed Cochrane."

"Of course! That's what I said at first. That I fired twice after he fell. And then you said there were three bullets fired from my gun and I— Oh!" She caught herself up suddenly, staring at the three empty brass cylinders in front of the captain. "But—if there were only three shots fired altogether—"

"And there are three bullets missing from your pistol," Rodriquiz put in pleasantly.

Carmela winced, looking dazed and disbelieving. "I don't understand. It's all so sort of mixed up."

"Wait a minute," Shayne said. "That's a six-shooter, isn't it? Why are there only five shells?"

"That's all I ever put in it," Carmela told him. "Father taught me to keep an empty chamber under the hammer."

"The three exploded cartridges were in a row behind the one empty chamber," Captain Rodriquiz agreed. "Would it not be better to tell the truth, Miss Towne? A full confession. He insulted you, perhaps? To defend your honor, you were forced to fire the shot."

"But I didn't!" Carmela cried wildly. "Someone else shot him and ran away in the darkness. That's the way it happened." She clamped her lips together and settled back to fight for composure.

Shayne said, "I think you'd better tell us why you are over here tonight. Why you met Neil Cochrane in *El Gato Pobre* and were going to a place like Papa Tonto's with him."

"He was taking me to Lance. He said he was. He swore Lance was at that awful place. He and Father both said so."

"Wait a minute," said Shayne. "Take your time and tell us all about it. When did Cochrane tell you that?"

"This afternoon. After Father came home from— after he was released. Neil came to see him. They were in the library arguing violently when I passed to go upstairs. I heard Lance's name mentioned as I went by. I jerked the door open and demanded to know what they were talking about—what about Lance. But Father wouldn't let me stay. He ordered me out. He was angrier than I've ever seen him.

"I went up to my room and waited until Neil left," she went on in a hard, strained voice. "Then I went down and confronted Father. I demanded to know what Neil had been saying about Lance. He refused to tell me, at first. He insisted it would be better if I didn't know. But I threatened to leave home unless he told me. I accused him of trying to keep us apart again as he did once before.

"Then Father exploded. He said, all right. That I might as well know the truth. He said he'd paid Neil to keep quiet about it so I wouldn't find out. That that's what the argument was about and Neil had demanded money for his silence. Then he told me Lance was mixed up in some Nazi spy activities and he was making his headquarters here at a place called Papa Tonto's.

"I didn't believe it," Carmela went on rapidly, her cheeks beginning to show a little color. "I accused Father of lying to keep me away from Lance. And he cursed me and said, all right, if I wanted proof why didn't I get Neil to show me. I told him I would. That I'd call Neil up and ask him. And he said he'd paid Neil to promise not to tell me, and that Neil would probably deny it if I asked him, but why not get him to take me to Papa Tonto's so I could see for myself.

"And that's what I did," she ended dully. "I called Neil and asked him if he'd take me to Papa Tonto's tonight, and offered to meet him at *El Gato Pobre* after dinner. So we did, but when I asked him about Lance he denied everything—because Father had paid him to, I guess. He wouldn't believe me when I said Father had told me the truth. But he was willing enough to take me. He didn't seem to think that was breaking his promise to Father. And that's—all. We were almost there when—it happened."

Shayne asked, "He did insult you, didn't he?"

She shrugged disdainfully. "He made some horrid remarks. He pretended to think I had asked him to take me to that place because I *wanted* to. You know, because I wanted *him* to take me there. I don't know what kind of a place it is, but from what he said I guess women do go there with men."

Shayne said, "Listen carefully now: When you went into *El Gato Pobre,* where was Cochrane?"

"Dancing with a girl. He took her back to another table where there were two men, while I waited just inside the door."

"Did you recognize the girl?"

Carmela caught her lower lip between her teeth and looked frightened for the first time. "How do you know all about it?"

"Captain Rodriquiz and I were there watching. Did you recognize the girl, Carmela?"

"All right. I did," she flashed at him. "It was the same one I saw with Lance in El Paso. The one whose picture you showed me the other night."

Shayne nodded grimly. "Did you ask Cochrane about her?"

"Yes. He just laughed and said she was one of the habituées of Papa Tonto's whom he knew slightly."

"And when you left the restaurant," Shayne persisted, "did you notice the girl ahead of you?"

"Yes, I did. She and the two men with her. They stayed ahead of us all the way, and Neil said they were probably going to Papa Tonto's too."

Captain Rodriquiz had been following Shayne's questions and Carmela's answers with alert interest. He now interposed, "And when you turned into the alley, were they not ahead of you still?"

"I think so. Yes. I saw them just ahead when the clouds cleared for a moment."

"And after the first shot was fired?" Rodriquiz persisted.

"It was so dark. And I was excited and confused."

"Why did you bring that gun with you tonight?" Shayne asked suddenly.

"Well, I was going to that dreadful place with Neil Cochrane. And Father suggested it. In fact, he refused to let me out unless I promised to bring it. I think he was afraid something might happen."

A Mexican policeman came in and saluted briskly, laying a little wad of cotton on the desk in front of Rodriquiz. A misshapen lump of lead lay on top of the cotton. He spoke briefly in Spanish and went out.

The captain lifted the bullet and weighed it in his fingers for a moment. He nodded gravely, and passed it to Shayne. "It is the death bullet. Of thirty-eight caliber, I think."

Shayne leaned forward to take it. Carmela's eyes

were fixed on it in fascination. Shayne tested its weight as had the captain, and agreed, "It's about the right weight." He inspected it closely, "Impossible to get a decent ballistics test, the way it mushroomed against a bone."

"The way it is flattened," said Rodriquiz firmly, "is most important, I think."

Shayne nodded. He told Carmela, "That's what happens to a bullet when it's been notched like those in your gun."

She shrank away from him. "I didn't shoot him, Michael. I swear I didn't."

"But your gun did."

"How do you know? You just said it couldn't be tested by ballistics, the way it's flattened out. That's the only way to prove it was fired from my gun, isn't it?"

"Even if it wasn't mushroomed," Shayne growled, "there isn't enough rifling in that sawed-off barrel to make a conclusive test. But we can easily enough prove it's the right caliber—and any expert will swear it was notched like yours before it was fired. There were only three shots fired, Carmela. And three bullets have been fired from your gun. For God's sake," he went on hoarsely, "don't bury your face in the sand. This is murder. You can fry for it just the same as anyone else if you don't tell the truth. *Who fired your pistol the first time, if you didn't?*"

She shook her head defiantly. "No one. It was in my bag when that first shot was fired."

"That's a lousy story," Shayne groaned. "All the facts are against you. You can beat the rap by admitting you killed him. Hell, Cochrane was a skunk. He'd lured you into this trip to Papa Tonto's, the worst kind of a dive. You wouldn't have any trouble making a jury believe you had a hell of a good reason for killing him."

"But I didn't!" she cried fiercely.

"All right. Then you're lying to protect the one who did," Shayne told her coldly. "That's the only other answer that fits the facts."

"I want a lawyer," she said suddenly. "You told me I didn't have to answer without a lawyer to advise me."

Shayne nodded glumly. "You'll have a chance to think it over tonight." He looked at Rodriquiz. "I suppose you'll hold her."

The captain spread out his hands eloquently. "As you have said. With the facts we have, I cannot do otherwise."

"While you're thinking it over in a cell," Shayne told her harshly, "I'll be looking for Lance Bayliss. This isn't just one murder, Carmela. It's the third."

She stood up, averting her head proudly. "I'm ready, Captain."

He leaped to his feet and opened the door for her. He returned a few minutes later and reseated himself with a sigh. "You have a theory, Mr. Shayne?"

"No. Only that this is hooked up somehow with two other recent murders in El Paso." Shayne scowled across the room. "Haven't they picked up Marquita and her soldiers yet?"

"They are bringing Marquita in for questioning. Her companions have not been found. The girl was arrested a few minutes ago in her room a few blocks from Papa Tonto's."

Shayne gave him a description of Lance Bayliss. "You'd better get out a pick-up for him. I don't know how he figures in this, but I'm afraid his alibi for the time of the murder may be important."

"He is—the sweetheart of Miss Towne?"

"He was. Long ago." Shayne rumpled his red hair angrily. "He's the only person mixed up in any of this whom Carmela might protect."

"It is your opinion that this man used her gun?"

"It makes too much sense to please me," Shayne admitted. "Bayliss used to love Carmela, and he hated Cochrane's guts. If he was hiding in the alley tonight, it could have happened that way. I can imagine him attacking Cochrane, getting the worst of it in the scuffle, and Carmela opening her bag to get the gun and help him out. Whether he grabbed it and pulled the trigger, or whether she did—" He shook his head, glaring at the short-barreled weapon. "You'd better test it for fingerprints."

"I have touched it only by the trigger-guard," Rodriquiz assured him. "If you wish to make the tests in your laboratories, I will be happy."

"Sure," Shayne agreed. "Reload it just as it was when you took it away from her. And I'll take this bullet along, if you want."

"It will be best." Rodriquiz carefully reloaded the revolver with both empty and full cartridges. "We have not the modern laboratory in Juarez."

A policeman came in with Cochrane's belongings

that had been found on his person. There was a key ring and some loose change, a leather billfold, and a telegram in its yellow envelope. The billfold had an assortment of business cards and $67 in bills. The telegram had been sent that day from Mexico City. It read: *Legal title to Plata Azul passed to Señora Telgucado on death of husband to be held in trust during her lifetime for legal heirs. — Aguido Valverde.*

Marquita Morales was ushered into the office while they were puzzling over the telegram. She had washed most of the rouge from her face, and changed from her black dress to a blouse and wool skirt. She looked young and frightened, and she loosed a torrent of questions in her own language at the captain as soon as she was inside the room.

Shayne couldn't follow the conversation with his limited knowledge of Spanish, but the captain sternly quieted her and then proceeded with the questioning in English.

Marquita started by stating that she had been alone in her room all evening and hadn't the slightest idea why she had been arrested and dragged to police headquarters, but she began to sob and changed her story as soon as the captain informed her that she had been watched by American and Mexican police ever since she picked up the two soldiers in El Paso that afternoon.

She then admitted inducing the soldiers to come to Juarez with her, and taking them to a place where they could change clothes to cross the border unchallenged. They had dinner and a few drinks at *El Gato Pobre*, she said sullenly, but that was too tame for them and they insisted on going elsewhere.

Yes, to Papa Tonto's, she flashed at her questioner. Why not? It was what the stupid gringo *soldados* wanted. But when they were approaching the place through the alley, someone started shooting at them from behind. They were frightened, and they ran away from the bullets, she said simply. She didn't know where the soldiers went. She lost them in the darkness, and she hurried to her own room and bolted the door and stayed there until the police came.

Yes, she had noticed the American couple following her down the street from *El Gato Pobre,* but she didn't know why. She knew *Señor* Cochrane slightly, she admitted with a toss of her head and a defiant glance at Shayne, but she didn't know why he would follow her. She at first refused to admit he had spoken to her in the café, and then admitted the dance with him, and said that he had asked her if the two men at her table were soldiers, and he refused to believe her when she denied it. He warned her to be careful of trouble if they were soldiers, but she didn't think it was any of his business and told him so.

No, she hadn't seen anyone else in the alley except the couple behind her. There might have been someone hiding against the buildings in the darkness as they passed, she admitted, but they had seen no one. Their first intimation of trouble was when shots sounded behind them and bullets started whizzing over their heads.

Then they ran so fast that if there was anyone else

running behind them, she didn't think they would have known it.

Captain Rodriquiz shrugged and gave up the questioning with a glance at Shayne. The big redhead hunched forward and said, "You remember me, don't you, Marquita?"

"*Sí*, I theenk you are in ze police office in El Paso."

"How many soldiers have you brought over to Papa Tonto's this way?" Shayne demanded.

"No others," she insisted. "I 'ave heard ees easy for do, so I try tonight."

"Who told you about it?"

She shrugged. Some of the other girls in Juarez. It was a common practice, she said.

"Who pays the girls to do it?" Shayne demanded. "Who talks to the soldiers when they get doped up at Papa Tonto's?"

She began to cry, and whimpered that she didn't understand. No one paid them—except the soldiers themselves. They went to Tonto's "—for to 'ave one good time." She insisted she knew no more about it than that.

"When did you visit your mother last?" Shayne asked abruptly.

She looked up in surprise and said, "Las' Sunday I am see her."

"Did she talk to you about Mr. Towne? Tell you when she expected him to visit her again?"

She made her eyes very wide and round and repeated, "Mr. Towne?" as though she had never heard the name before. And no amount of questioning from

Shayne or the Mexican police captain would make her admit any knowledge of an affair between her mother and Mr. Towne. If she did know about it, she had been well-coached to deny it.

Rodriquiz ordered her locked up after the questioning was over, and after she was taken away, he admitted to Shayne, "I can keep her in jail one night only. She has broken no laws of Mexico in what she has done."

Shayne grimaced and admitted, "I'm not sure whether she has broken any American laws either, though I'm quite sure Military Intelligence will want to question her tomorrow." He got up wearily. "I appreciate all your help, and I'll get in touch with you tomorrow."

"And Miss Towne?" Rodriquiz asked politely. "What statement shall I give the reporters?"

"Tell the truth," Shayne advised. "That you're holding her on suspicion of murder until she satisfactorily explains who fired the first shot from her pistol. To cover yourself, you might add that you suspect her of protecting the person who actually fired the shot." Shayne went out and got in his borrowed car and drove back across the International Bridge.

CHAPTER TWENTY

It was almost midnight, and Jefferson Towne's house was dark when Shayne stopped out in front. He went up the steps and held the electric button down as he had done the preceding night. As before, he faintly heard chimes echoing through the silent mansion.

After a long time the light came on over his head. He took his finger off the button and listened to the inside bolt being thrown and the night-chain loosened.

Towne's Mexican butler stood in front of him, blocking the entrance, when the door opened. He wore a woolen bathrobe, with his bare legs showing below it and with Mexican sandals on his feet. He grunted, "W'at you want?"

"Towne." Shayne moved forward.

The Mexican gave way before him reluctantly. "I do not think—"

Shayne said, "Call him down here or I'll start hunting."

The Mexican turned to go up the stairs, shaking his head and muttering to himself. Shayne stayed behind in the big hallway. He didn't have to wait long before Jefferson Towne appeared at the head of the stairs and called down irritably, "Shayne? What the devil do you want?"

He wore a brocade dressing gown over yellow silk

pajamas. His hair was tousled and he scowled angrily down at the detective. Shayne sauntered toward the foot of the stairs, saying pleasantly, "I thought you might like to know that your daughter is in the Juarez jail charged with murder."

Towne said hoarsely, "Carmela? Murder?" He started down, planting each foot solidly and heavily on the succeeding steps. "What are you talking about, Shayne?"

"Murder," the detective repeated implacably. "Don't act so surprised. You must have expected something like that when you sent her over to the worst dive in Juarez with a man-killing pistol in her bag."

Towne stopped three steps above him. One hand gripped the banister tightly. "Who? What happened? For God's sake, man, speak up!"

"Don't pull an act on me," Shayne growled. "You knew what might happen when she went over there. You advised her to pack that sawed-off cannon with her. And then you calmly went to bed. You must have had a hunch she wouldn't be back tonight," he probed fiercely. "The door was barred and chained so she couldn't get in."

"She has her key to the side door," Towne mumbled. His rugged face was flaccid for a brief moment, and his big body appeared to shrink before Shayne's hard gaze. Then he got hold of himself and went on angrily: "Whatever happened is the result of her own stubbornness. She *would* go to see for herself. Who's dead? How did it happen?" He descended the last three steps, and his eyes were level with Shayne's.

"A bullet out of her gun killed Neil Cochrane."

"Cochrane?" The name seemed to surprise Towne more than Shayne's blunt announcement of her predicament.

"Cochrane," Shayne repeated. "Who did you expect her to kill when you let her go off like that?"

"I don't know," Towne confessed. "Somehow, I thought of Bayliss. How did it happen? Why the devil did she turn on Cochrane?"

Shayne shrugged his broad shoulders. "She claims she didn't do it." He hesitated. "Did you see her gun before she started out?"

"No. But she promised me she'd take it with her."

"How lately have you seen it?" Shayne persisted.

"I don't know. It's been years since I thought of it. What's that got to do with it, Shayne?"

"The only way she can beat the rap is by proving the gun held an empty cartridge before she started out. Which I don't believe," he went on frankly. "All three cartridges appear to be freshly fired."

"Wait a minute," Towne protested. "You're talking in riddles." He moved past Shayne toward the library, muttering, "I need a drink."

"I can use one myself." Shayne followed him inside the somber room.

Towne went directly to a built-in cabinet beside the fireplace and opened it. He stooped and got a tall bottle and two thin-stemmed goblets. He poured bonded *tequila* into both glasses and handed one to Shayne. He seemed dazed and unsure of himself, as though he was just awakening to the full seriousness of Shayne's

news. He tilted his glass and drank it down as though
he enjoyed it, breathing gustily as he finished.

Shayne grimaced at the odor rising from his glass
but tried a gulp of the Mexican liquor. To his surprise,
it wasn't half bad. Towne poured himself some more,
and set the bottle down on a table in front of Shayne.
He said, "Suppose you tell me what happened."

"The Mexican police can give you all the details.
From all the evidence at present, one of those lovely,
homemade dumdums from Carmela's thirty-eight killed
Cochrane in the alley leading to Papa Tonto's. Carmela
declares she fired twice at some vague form running
away in the darkness *after* Cochrane was killed. But
three bullets have been fired from her gun. Only three
shots were fired altogether. One of them killed Cochrane."

"If they find the bullet, can't they compare it with
one fired from her gun?" Towne asked eagerly.

"A dumdum?" Shayne snorted. "Fired from a gun
with less than half an inch of rifling? Not a chance in
the world of getting a decent comparison."

"You think she's lying?" Towne muttered.

Shayne said, "It looks as though she might have recognized the man lurking in the alley who grabbed her
pistol and shot Cochrane—and is covering up for him."

"Then that can mean only one man," Towne pointed
out. "Lance Bayliss. And he's mixed up in some crooked
work, Shayne. Neil Cochrane came here this afternoon
and threatened to tell Carmela the whole story if I
didn't pay him to keep it quiet."

"And you paid him?" Shayne asked curiously.

"I promised to. What else could I do? Carmela still loves the man. I couldn't see her hurt."

"That's quite a change of heart," Shayne snorted. "Ten years ago, when Lance was decent, you broke her heart by separating them."

"She was too young to know what she wanted. I distrusted the fellow. And rightly, too. You can see that now. Her life would have been like hell if she had married him."

Shayne finished his *tequila*. He set his glass down and asked, "What is the English translation for *plata azul?*"

Towne looked at Shayne as though he thought he had lost his senses. "*Plata azul?* Blue silver. Silver blue, actually, but the Mexicans put their adjectives behind—"

"I know," Shayne said impatiently. "Does that have any particular meaning to you?"

"There's a silver mine in Mexico by that name. I don't know—"

"What about *Señora* Telgucado?" Shayne interrupted.

"What about her? What the hell are you getting at, Shayne?"

"I don't know," the detective admitted. "But I hope to before long." He turned on his heel and started to walk out.

"Wait a minute!" Towne hurried after him. "I want to talk to you about this, Shayne. About Carmela. We'll have to find Lance Bayliss. You can name your own price—"

Shayne kept on going toward the front door. He flung over his shoulder, "I expect to name my own price, Towne. And you're going to be damned glad to pay it." He went out the door and pulled it shut behind him.

He got into his car and drove away, swinging east to avoid the business section and to hit the highway leading down into the Rio Grande Valley—and on toward the Big Bend and a closely guarded silver mine from which Jefferson Towne had taken a fortune in the past ten years.

CHAPTER TWENTY-ONE

Michael Shayne began slowing down when he approached the intersection of the road from Marfa to the Lone Star mine. He was still a good mile from the locked gates that had kept him out the other time, but he pulled to the side of the mountain road on the other side of the intersection, swung around in a sharp U-turn, cut off his motor, and left the coupé parked with its headlights pointing downhill on the road over which he had just driven.

After taking a flashlight from the glove compartment and a pair of heavy wire cutters from the floor, he switched off the headlights, left the keys in the ignition, and got out to trudge up the road beside the spur track toward the silver mine. Brisk, long-legged strides brought him to the padlocked gates in less than fifteen minutes. He stopped in the road when he saw the heavy galvanized wire glistening in the moonlight.

Peering ahead intently, Shayne could make out the blurred outline of the guard shack, but there was no light in it. Beyond, where he knew the mining camp lay, there was only the light of the moon.

He didn't take a chance on the gates being totally unguarded at night, but turned to the left of the road, pushing through the underbrush and climbing the steep slope for a hundred yards before circling over to strike the woven wire barrier. With his heavy cutters he started carefully snipping a large hole in the fence.

When the hole was large enough to go through easily, he laid the cutters down and entered Jefferson Towne's carefully protected border property, pausing for a moment to take his bearings. He then strode forward boldly on a course that intercepted the wooden ore chute between the headframe and the bin below where railroad cars received their loads of pay dirt.

He followed the chute up the hillside toward the steel headframe outlined starkly against the horizon. He had only the vaguest idea of what he was looking for or hoped to accomplish. He knew only that a lot of fingers seemed to point toward this silver mine in the Big Bend.

His suspicions were aroused by the manner in which the place was guarded against strangers. The heavy fence and an armed guard at the padlocked gates just didn't make sense around a silver mine. His knowledge of mining was limited, but he knew that the ore itself wasn't very valuable until it was smelted, and he doubted whether such precautions had to be taken against border raiders.

He only hoped he would know what he was looking for when he found it. With his scant knowledge, he should have brought an expert along, but he didn't know any experts in El Paso, and it might prove embarrassing to let anyone in on his hunch until it was proved correct

A hundred feet below the headframe over the original shaft, the chute ended abruptly at another huge storage bin similar to the one below where the cars were loaded. But this bin sat flush with the ground, with the chute leading out from the lower end. Shayne circled it and discovered that the ore chute did not extend beyond the very edge of a crater-like depression not unlike a huge gravel pit that has been in use for a number of years.

He could see the gaunt outlines of two steam shovels squatting in the bottom of the pit, and a long boom slanted upward from the bottom to the edge of the bin over his head. With his flashlight, he turned a beam upward onto the boom and saw a long line of elevating-buckets on an endless chain that was evidently used to carry material up from the pit and dump it into the storage bin at the top of the gravity chute.

He turned off the flash and squatted beside the bin to mull over his discovery. There was no doubt that the original shaft and its headframe had long since been abandoned as a source of ore, and he remembered the mistake which Josiah Riley had supposedly made in reporting that the original vein had pinched out.

To Shayne, totally unversed in such things, it was clear that the present mining procedure consisted in the use of steam shovels in the bottom of the huge pit digging out the entire hillside and sending the muck up to the bin, where it was fed down by gravity into railroad cars below.

This seemed to indicate that Riley's report on the original vein might have been correct; and now, instead of sinking a new shaft and driving new tunnels into the mountain, Towne was simply scraping the surface for his loads of rich ore that went into his El Paso smelter every day.

Shayne squatted on his heels and lit a cigarette, carefully shielding the match and the glow from the direction of the silent camp below. He wished to God he knew more about hard-rock mining. This seemed to him an unorthodox way to operate a silver mine, but he didn't know that it *couldn't* be done that way. It was a revolutionary method, at least, he finally decided. If Jefferson Towne had worked out a secret process for extracting valuable ore from the side of a mountain, it wasn't surprising that he took such precautions to keep it a secret.

He finished his cigarette and decided that it was not worthwhile to explore any more. He didn't yet know the full meaning of his discovery, but he had learned all he could for the night. He stood up and retraced his steps down the hillside, found his hole in the fence, and proceeded on to his car without being challenged.

Daylight was approaching when he started back to El Paso, and the sun had been up more than an hour when he pulled up in front of the Paso Del Norte Hotel.

He went up to his room and began stripping off his clothes. He was physically weary, but his mind was working furiously as he went over hypothesis after hypothesis, rejecting one after the other. He had an irritating, nagging feeling of being on the verge of an answer to the mysterious deaths of three men, but the final piece in the pattern, the *reason* behind it all, continued to elude him.

He shaved and took a shower, then came back into

the room clad only in undershirt and shorts, and poured a long drink. Sitting by the window with the drink in his hand, he scowled out at the bright sunlight. There it was—the answer—just in front of him, but he couldn't see it. The image dimmed each time he tried to take hold of it and examine it objectively.

A knock sounded on his door as he took a long drink of whisky. He got up and padded toward it in his bare feet, and pulled it open. Lance Bayliss pushed past him into the center of the room. He carried a morning paper and a briefcase and his face was strained and terrified. He dropped the briefcase and turned to demand hoarsely, "Is this stuff in the paper about Carmela true?"

Shayne closed the door and said, "I haven't seen the paper, Lance, but I imagine it's fairly correct."

"That she's in that filthy Juarez jail! Accused of murdering Neil Cochrane!" He struck the paper with his free hand.

"That's about it." Shayne walked over and picked up the whisky bottle and asked, "Have a drink?"

"You helped put her there," Lance charged. "It says in the paper you're one of the witnesses against her—that you're convinced she did it."

"That her *gun* did it," Shayne corrected. "It's my personal theory that she's shielding someone—that she'll probably go to the electric chair shielding him." His eyes met Lance's and held them steadily.

Lance drew in a long breath. "It also says the police have reason to believe I was in that vicinity last night."

"Carmela placed you there herself. *She* thinks you were there, Lance."

Bayliss dropped the paper to the floor and said, "All right. I was there. I grabbed the gun and killed Cochrane. I didn't think she recognized me in the dark."

CHAPTER TWENTY-TWO

Shayne poured a drink and handed it to Lance. He asked, "Why did you kill Cochrane?"

Bayliss gulped down a big drink and said, "I guess I went crazy for a moment." He walked over to the window and stared out, his back turned to Shayne, and continued. "I suppose it was seeing her with that rat—going to that foul dive with him. I've dreamed about her for ten years, Shayne—of coming back to her. I had an idea, God help me, she'd be the same."

"Why didn't you go in to see her the night you went to the house—when she was alone and waiting for you?"

Lance turned slowly, the muscles in his thin face quivering. "What do you know about it?"

"I saw you parked in the street in front of the house. You drove away as I passed."

"So that was you—with the spotlight," Lance said. "I parked there for an hour trying to get up enough nerve to go in. I didn't know whether she'd want to see me or not. I've changed a lot myself."

Shayne sat down on the bed and sipped his drink thoughtfully, then asked, "What were you doing in that Juarez alley last night?"

"Does that matter?" Lance answered irritably. "I was

there. I grabbed her gun and killed Cochrane with it."
He slumped into a chair. "You suspected me all along,
didn't you? You knew I'd give myself up when I read
the newspaper story and realized it was the only way to
save her."

"I knew that's what you would have done ten years
ago. But why did you kill him?"

"I've told you."

"You gave me an answer that'll sound good enough
in court," Shayne agreed. "I'd like the truth."

"Why don't you take me in?" Bayliss said roughly.
He clamped his lips, and looked at the drink in his
hand.

"There are still two other deaths to be accounted
for," Shayne reminded him.

"What do they matter now? I'll hang for killing
Cochrane. Forget the others."

"I think they were all committed by the same
person."

"I didn't come here to talk about any other murders.
I gave myself up to you instead of the cops because I
hoped I could make a deal."

"What sort of deal?"

"I told you I was doing some undercover work. I've
picked up a lot of stuff that should be turned over to
the FBI, or the army. The police might not pay any
attention to a confessed murderer. I hoped you would,
Shayne."

"What kind of stuff? Activities of foreign agents?"

"I thought that's what it was at first," Lance said

despondently. "But it isn't that important. There's a ring operating in El Paso that makes a business of encouraging soldiers to desert the army, and smuggles them into the interior of Mexico for a thousand bucks a head."

Shayne said, "I'll see that your information is used. Who heads the ring?"

"That's one of the favors I wanted to ask of you. Will you arrange to put off the round-up until after the election?"

Shayne's gaunt face hardened. "Manny Holden and Honest John Carter?"

Lance Bayliss flung out his hands. "I've got to trust you with it now." He finished his drink and set the glass on the floor. "I've got enough dope to put them both in Federal prison. All I ask is that you hold off until Carter is elected, then spring it. If we make it public now, Jefferson Towne will be elected mayor. Wait until he's defeated."

Shayne said, "Towne would make El Paso a good mayor."

"We went over that once before," Lance said. "He's dangerous, Shayne. You don't realize how he sees himself. Give him this first political triumph, and God knows where he'll stop."

"I won't promise anything. Turn your information over to me and I'll use it as I see fit."

"It's here in my briefcase," Lance muttered.

Shayne asked, "Is a Mexican girl named Marquita Morales mixed up in the deal?"

Lance looked surprised. "You do get around, don't you?" he said. "I don't think so—not knowingly, at least. I suspected her when I learned she helped soldiers get a change of clothes to cross the border in. But that's only a small sideline of the ring."

"Did you ever talk to Marquita about her mother?" Shayne asked.

"Her mother? I didn't know she had a mother." Lance got up and stood before Shayne to demand, "Come on —take me in. What are we waiting for? Carmela will be released as soon as I give myself up, won't she?"

"As soon as your story is checked," Shayne corrected him. He began pulling on his trousers. "I'll go down to headquarters with you."

Thirty minutes later they entered Chief Dyer's office, to find him fuming over a news item which he held in his hand. "What's this about Cochrane and the Towne girl?" he stormed at Shayne. "Why the devil didn't you notify me last night? By God, I have to read the papers to find out what's happening around here."

"That's a headache for the Juarez police," Shayne reminded him. "Chief, this is Lance Bayliss. He's giving himself up for the murder of Neil Cochrane. I'll let you take care of getting him across the border where he belongs."

Chief Dyer started barking astonished questions, and Lance Bayliss answered them firmly.

It was half an hour later before Shayne and the police chief were again alone in Dyer's office. The chief fitted a cigarette into his long holder and tilted it

.....een his teeth. "You've suspected this Bayliss fellow of having a hand in things all along," he charged.

Shayne said, "He was in and out of it all the way. Frankly, I thought he might be mixed up in some Nazi spying activities."

"There's still a lot of his story not told," Dyer said. "I figure he just came to the end of his rope on Cochrane and gave himself up to save the girl. We'll sweat the rest of it out of him, all right."

"He's holding a lot back," Shayne agreed. "By the way, I left the death gun with ballistics for a report last night. Has it come in?"

"Not yet. I don't see that we need it now."

Shayne said, "It might be important." He changed the subject abruptly. "Ever hear of the *Plata Azul* mine in Mexico?"

Dyer nodded with a look of surprise. "One of Jeff Towne's properties. A white elephant, from what I hear."

"What do you hear?"

"The *Free Press* carried a write-up about it a month or so ago," Dyer recalled. "Taking Towne to task for investing capital earned in this country in a worthless Mexican mine. Seems he's a stubborn cuss and has been pouring money into it for ten years without getting anything out, installing a modern stamp mill and keeping a big crew at work without producing anything. Mining men are apt to be like that. Make a fortune out of one mine, and put it all back into another hole in the ground."

"Where's the *Plata Azul* located?" Shayne asked tensely.

"Chihuahua, I think. About a hundred miles northwest of Ojinaga."

"How close to the border is that?"

"Not so far from the Big Bend. Queerest part of it, as the *Free Press* pointed out, is why an American wants to fool with looking for Mexican silver when our government pays a subsidy on American silver making it worth almost twice as much."

Shayne settled back with a frown. "Say that again."

"Sure." Chief Dyer was relaxed and discursive, with Lance Bayliss safely in jail. "One of the New Deal boondoggles still in effect. I think it was back in 1934 when they raised the price of raw domestic silver to about seventy cents, leaving the price of foreign stuff at thirty-five or thereabouts. It was a big help to the western miners even if the rest of the country did have to pay the difference out of tax money."

"I don't quite get it," Shayne argued. "Do you mean our government pays more per ounce for silver mined in this country than if it comes from abroad?"

"That's it. Every ounce that goes to the mint has to be accompanied by proof that it's freshly mined, and of its source. Government investigators are on the job checking shipments all the time. Our department has cooperated in running down a couple of operators trying to slip Mexican silver across and pretend it was mined in this country."

Shayne was sitting erect, listening alertly. He leaned

back now and massaged his left earlobe between his fingers. His rugged features held a queer, brooding look of expectancy. Chief Dyer puffed on his cigarette and watched him for a moment, then asked, "Have you anything that ties Bayliss in with the other two deaths we've been investigating?"

"All of them have to tie together," growled Shayne. "Find out *why* Cochrane was bumped, and you'll have the answer to the other two."

"Bayliss says—"

"He lies," Shayne told him wearily. "He hadn't seen Carmela Towne for ten years. He's been around El Paso for weeks without getting in touch with her. He didn't commit murder last night just because she was out with another man."

"Why, then?"

Shayne wasn't listening to him any longer. The brooding look went away from his face, and he became grim and alert. He muttered, "I've been wondering how I was going to earn my expenses up here— May I use your phone?" He reached for it without waiting for the chief to answer, called Jefferson Towne's number.

The Mexican butler answered. Shayne asked for Towne, and waited. After a few moments, he said, "This is Mike Shayne, Towne. Have you heard the news?"

He lifted one eyebrow at Dyer as he listened for a moment, then he chuckled and explained, "Lance Bayliss has confessed using Carmela's gun on Cochrane last night. That's right. Thought you'd be interested."

He listened a moment, and then his voice and expression hardened: "You've still got an election to win in two weeks. Remember what I told you last night? That you'd be glad to pay me my own price? This is it. Listen carefully, because I'm just going to say it once: I have in my possession information that will put both John Carter and Manny Holden behind bars if and when I turn it over to the Federal authorities. I'm the only man who has that dope or even knows about it. It's the only thing that will beat Carter at the polls the way things stand now. If you don't want to buy it, I'm sure Holden will."

Pausing to listen, Shayne glanced across the desk at Dyer, who glared at him with amazement and anger ludicrously mingled on his naked face.

"That's the way it stands," Shayne said into the telephone. "How much is it worth to you for me to spring it before the election? Sure, it's blackmail," he chuckled. "You should be used to that by now. You paid Jack Barton ten grand to keep him quiet about something that would defeat you. Another ten grand won't break you."

He waited for a moment, then said harshly, "I don't trust you either. This is going to be an open-and-shut sale, with everything on top of the table. I've got something you want to buy. I'll sell it for ten G's and let you look it over to satisfy yourself it's the McCoy before you make payment.

"We'll do it at your house in two hours," he went on sharply. "I'm catching a plane to New Orleans at noon. Do we deal? Or do I have to sell it to Holden and Carter?" He listened again, then said, "Right. In two hours. Have the money ready." He hung up, and grinned at Dyer. "Now you know how a private dick manages to earn a living in these hard times."

"Damn it, Shayne," Dyer roared, "are you serious about this thing? Have you got such information?"

"I haven't looked at it yet," Shayne told him, "but I'm pretty sure it's on the level."

"And you would deliberately keep it out of the hands of the authorities unless Towne paid you for it? I know your reputation for pulling fast ones, Shayne, but I've always heard you played fair with justice in the end."

"Maybe I wouldn't have held it out," Shayne argued good-naturedly. "Maybe I was going to turn it over to you anyway. Isn't justice going to be served this way just as well? And I'll net ten grand out of it."

Before Dyer could reply, Shayne went on briskly: "Did you ever get a report from Washington on the fingerprints of that drowned boy? Or find out anything about Jack Barton in California, or anywhere between here and California on the bus?"

"There hasn't been time on the fingerprints," Dyer told him, "and so far we haven't located Barton."

"I'd like a set of those prints." Shayne's gray eyes were very bright. "And I've got to make a trip to the marriage-license bureau. Where is it?"

"Marriage-license bureau?" Dyer raged. "You're not—"

"No," Shayne said blithely, "I'm not. Where is the bureau?"

"Look here," said Dyer heavily, "about that information you say you have against Carter and Holden.

Suppose Towne refused to pay you for it at the show-down? How do I know you won't go to Holden for your ten grand?"

"You don't," Shayne admitted with a grin.

"I can't let you play around with important evidence like that for your personal profit," Dyer sputtered. "Where is it?"

Shayne said, "I've got it in a safe place."

"*What* is it? What have you got on Holden and Carter?"

Shayne shook his head. "I've got to do some bargaining first."

"You're compounding a felony by holding out such evidence."

"Don't worry about that. Towne will rush it to you as soon as he gets his hands on it."

"But you threatened to take it to Holden if Towne doesn't pay off. *He* won't turn it over to me."

"That's right," Shayne agreed. "But Towne knows that, too, and that's why he'll have to deal with me."

"Give it to me first," Dyer urged him. "Keep the documents, or whatever they are, to sell to whoever wants to buy them. But let me have enough information to act on if anything goes wrong. That way, you play both ends against the middle."

"The stuff is valuable to me only so long as I have the exclusive decision as to how it shall be used," Shayne argued good-naturedly. "Towne wouldn't pay out a dime if he knew you already had the dope and were going to use it against Carter whether or not *he* buys it."

"But Towne doesn't have to know it's already in my

possession," Dyer pointed out. "I won't double-cross you. Make any sort of crooked deal you want, but cover yourself by giving it to me first."

"But that wouldn't be playing it fair," Shayne said blandly. "This way, I'm actually giving him something for his ten G's." He stood up and yawned. "Where did you say the license bureau was?"

CHAPTER TWENTY-THREE

Michael Shayne's first stop was at the police laboratory, where he picked up a set of fingerprints taken from the unidentified body found floating in the river, and got a report from ballistics on the bullet taken from Cochrane's body and Carmela's pistol.

The ballistics report was as meager and uninformative as he had feared after viewing the bullet and gun last night. The smashed condition of the bullet, together with the lack of rifling in the sawed-off .38, made it impossible to make a positive comparison to determine whether the death slug had been fired from that pistol or not. All the external evidence pointed to an affirmative answer, but the police experts would go no further than that. The three empty cartridges had been checked, however, and there was no difficulty in determining whether or not they had been fired from Carmela's gun.

From the laboratory, Shayne went to the marriage-license bureau, and he spent fifteen minutes going over old license records with the clerk. He was whistling cheerfully when he emerged from the City Hall and walked up the street to the police coupé parked in front of his hotel.

A shabby little man sauntered along the street behind him. He looked like a western rancher in for a holiday, and was intensely interested in the shop windows along the street. He loitered inconspicuously behind the detective while he was getting in his car, and Shayne watched him in the rear-view mirror as he pulled away. The little man continued to loiter, seemingly unaware of his departure. Shayne thought maybe he was wrong about him.

He drove directly out to Fort Bliss, and without too much difficulty was able to talk with the post adjutant. He introduced himself and explained his interest in the death of Private James Brown, and learned that the body had been given a military burial after all efforts to uncover his real identity had proved unavailing

Shayne kept his own council about the recruit's letter to his mother in New Orleans. He didn't think the army would appreciate his holding out that information all this time, and it didn't seem a good moment to broach the subject. After a brief discussion of the mystifying elements of the case, Shayne said, "I understand you sent a set of fingerprints taken from the body to Washington for possible identification. No luck there?"

The adjutant shook his head. "We didn't bury the body until the Washington report was received. We had his fingerprints on his enlistment papers, you know, and we sent them in as soon as Cleveland reported no such address as he had given."

Shayne asked, "May I have a set of those prints from his enlistment record?"

The adjutant didn't see why he couldn't, and he sent an orderly to get a set for the detective. Then he eagerly asked what angle Shayne was working on, and what hopes he had of identifying the dead body. Shayne told

him it was too theoretical as yet to talk about, but he
thought he could promise definite progress within a
few hours.

When he went out to his car with Jimmie Delray's
fingerprints in his pocket, he saw a taxi parked half a
dozen cars back of his coupé. The shabby little man
whom he had last seen loitering in front of the Paso
Del Norte was inconspicuously shrunk down in the
back seat of the taxi.

Shayne grinned to himself as he drove off. He hadn't
been mistaken after all. He drove straight to his hotel
and went up to his room. Lance Bayliss's briefcase was
still in the closet where he and Lance had placed it
earlier. It lacked half an hour of his appointment with
Jefferson Towne. He opened the briefcase on his bed
and looked through the documentary evidence Lance
had promised was there.

It was very complete, with names and dates and
facts. Lance Bayliss had made a thorough investigation
of the business of smuggling deserters across the
border into the interior of Mexico. Larimer's secondhand clothing store was one of three such places in
El Paso that specialized in furnishing civilian outfits to
the deserters. The registration cards and other identification papers were forged in El Paso, and there was
documentary proof that Honest John Carter had been
allied with Holden as a financial backer in his pre-war
smuggling enterprises, and was continuing to take his
profit from this new angle.

Only one thing disappointed Shayne. Neil Cochrane's
name was mentioned several times in Lance's material,

but there was no evidence at all that the reporter had had any actual knowledge of what was going on.

Shayne sighed, and replaced the papers in the brief-case. It was dynamite, right enough. Plenty strong enough to blow Honest John Carter right out of the mayoralty race, leaving Towne unopposed.

Shayne sympathized with Lance's wish to keep the evidence under cover until after the election. If it wasn't made public until after Carter was elected, he would simply be removed from office and someone else would be appointed to serve out his term in accord with city statutes. Any danger of Towne's filling the po-sition would be definitely eliminated. Knowing Lance's bitter hatred for Towne, Shayne could understand why he wanted the information handled that way. But if he waited until Towne was elected, the stuff wouldn't be worth a penny to the new mayor. *Before* election, it was easily worth ten thousand dollars to him. It was as simple as that.

Shayne poured himself a drink, and put a gun in his coat pocket. He tossed off the liquor, picked up the briefcase, and went out. He didn't bother to look around for the shabby little man as he drove off to keep his appointment with Towne. It was unlikely that they would bother to tail him any farther.

He didn't have to wait at Towne's front door this time. The Mexican butler recognized him with a nod and led the way back to the library. Towne was standing in front of the fireplace with his hands clasped behind his back. He nodded with a scowl, his gaze going to the briefcase Shayne carried. "That the stuff you described over the telephone?"

Shayne said, "This is it. Guaranteed to knock Carter out of the race." He set the briefcase down on a table, put his big hand up warningly when Towne stepped forward. "Let me see your end of the deal before you look at mine."

Towne laughed shortly. "I had to answer some embarrassing questions at the bank this morning when I drew out this second ten thousand." He drew an envelope from his pocket, opened it to riffle a sheaf of bills before Shayne. "When the police investigated the money I drew out for Barton, they practically told the bank it was for blackmail," he went on bitterly.

Shayne said, "If you lived right, you wouldn't be embarrassed by having to pay out blackmail." He nodded. "I'm satisfied. Look it over and see if you are." He unstrapped the briefcase and stepped back.

Towne replaced the money in his pocket and went to the briefcase. He took the papers out and began studying them eagerly. It was dark and gloomy inside the library, with the windows closed and half covered with dark drapes. Shayne strolled to one of the end windows and pulled the drapes back to let sunlight slant in. The windows were set in steel frames, opening on a rachet arrangement operated by a hand crank.

Shayne twisted the crank to open the window and let in a little fresh air. Towne was engrossed with the papers from Lance Bayliss's briefcase. Shayne leaned on the low windowsill and lit a cigarette. It was very quiet there on the hillside above the city, inside the big stone house set off from its neighbors by a thick box hedge.

Shayne smoked quietly for a time, and then asked without turning his head, "Are you satisfied it's what I promised you?"

"There's enough evidence to put Carter and Holden behind bars the rest of their lives," Towne told him exultantly. "I don't know how you dug this up, Shayne, but—"

"That doesn't matter." Shayne turned slowly. "Is it worth ten grand?"

"It's an outrageous holdup for me to pay you for this," Towne asserted angrily. "You could be jailed for trying to withhold this from the government."

Shayne nodded calmly, but his eyes held a dangerous glint. He dropped his right hand toward the gun sagging in his coat pocket and drawled, "You're not thinking of backing out, are you?"

"I never back out of a bargain," Towne said stiffly. He reached into his pocket for the envelope, tossed it toward Shayne. The detective caught it in his left hand. He opened it and took out the bills, fingered them lovingly while he counted the total.

"Okay," he said finally, straightening and replacing them in the envelope. He put the envelope in his left coat pocket and remained lounging back against the sill of the open window. "Now let's start talking about something important."

"I haven't anything else to discuss with you." Towne half turned away from him.

"We've got lots to talk about," Shayne corrected him gently. "Like the price of domestic silver—and the *Plata Azul* mine in Mexico."

Towne's wide shoulders stiffened. He turned slowly, and his eyes were murderous. "What do you know about the *Plata Azul?*"

"Practically everything," Shayne assured him. "When Cochrane was murdered last night, we found a telegram in his pocket from an attorney in Mexico City stating that title to the mine passed to a certain *Señora* Telgucado twenty-five years ago on the death of her husband —to be passed on to his heirs."

"Interesting," sneered Towne, "but hardly relevant."

"I think it is," Shayne insisted. "You see, I visited the marriage-license bureau this morning and confirmed a hunch. You and the widow of *Señor* Telgucado were married less than twenty-four years ago."

"It's a matter of record," Towne shrugged.

"But Carmela is almost thirty years old. That makes her your stepdaughter."

"Suppose she is my stepdaughter? I adopted her legally soon after we were married." Towne's voice was edged but restrained.

"She's still her father's legal heir," Shayne argued. "The *Plata Azul* mine legally reverted to her on her mother's death."

"Perhaps it did." Towne seemed uninterested. "While you were investigating my private affairs, you might have gone further to learn that I've been pouring money into that property for years without any returns. I was doing it for Carmela," he added, "hoping I could make a real strike and turn her over something worth while."

"Without her knowledge?"

"I've kept it for a surprise," Towne said stiffly. "What's your interest in it?"

"I'm interested in its proximity to the border—and the fact that Mexican silver is worth only half the price of domestic silver—plus the fact that Josiah Riley was fired from your employ ten years ago after reporting your vein in the Big Bend pinched out."

Towne's face was slowly being drained of color. "How do you figure those add up?"

"They add up to fraud," Shayne told him pleasantly, "when you consider the stamp mill you set up at the *Plata Azul* ten years ago, your ownership of a smelter here in El Paso where your Big Bend ore is processed, your revolutionary method of mining the Lone Star with steam shovels, and the fact that you went all out ten years ago to prevent Carmela from marrying the only man she ever wanted to marry."

"What do you know about the Lone Star mine?" Towne snarled.

"Everything. I paid the mine a visit last night, Towne. I know the shaft is abandoned, and for years you've been scooping up the mountainside to get bulk to load into cars on top of refined ore you've been smuggling over the border from the *Plata Azul*. By shipping it to your own smelter here, you've been able to hoodwink the government into paying you the double price for domestic silver. Not only that, but every ounce of it came from the Mexican mine actually owned by Carmela, and you've defrauded her out of a fortune during these ten years."

Towne stood very straight and very still in front of Shayne. "You sound very sure of your facts."

"It's the only answer that comes out right," Shayne said wearily. "It's tough, isn't it, after you got rid of Jack Barton and Neil Cochrane after they had discovered the truth? You thought your secret was safe. And now, by God, here's another guy popping up to plague you!"

Towne moved aside and sat down heavily in front of the liquor cabinet by the fireplace. He opened it and withdrew the *tequila* bottle they had drunk from last night. He poured himself a drink with a steady hand and asked, "What do you mean about Barton and Cochrane?"

Shayne glanced out the window into the sunlight. "After killing two men, it must be tough to learn your secret still isn't safe." He took a step forward away from the window.

Jefferson Towne stopped his glass two inches from his lips. He said stonily, "I paid Jack Barton, and I was prepared to meet Cochrane's price. I told him so yesterday afternoon. I can also afford to pay *you* off. How much?" He put the glass to his lips and drank.

Shayne shook his head and said mockingly, "Don't kid me, Towne. I know how your mind works. Josiah Riley inadvertently tipped me off with an old border proverb: '*Los muertos no hablan.*' You know it's cheaper to kill a man than to pay blackmail. The dead don't talk. That's the only sure way to shut up a blackmailer. That's why you killed Jack Barton Tuesday afternoon—and Cochrane last night."

Towne set his empty glass down. "Very interesting, except that you overlook a couple of facts. Jack Barton is in California spending the ten thousand I paid him—and I was in bed last night when Lance Bayliss shot Cochrane with Carmela's pistol."

Shayne shook his head. "Jack Barton never left for California. You bought a ticket and had someone get on the bus, just to make things look right if anyone checked up. And you drew the ten grand out of your bank and put one of them in the letter you had Jack write his parents before you killed him. But you should have had him address the envelope before you killed him, Towne. A man doesn't forget his own address, but *you* forgot to put *South* in front of the Vine Street number. That one mistake is what cooked your goose. The delay in the delivery of that letter sent the Bartons to Dyer with the whole story when they thought the unidentified body from the river was Jack."

"But it wasn't Barton!" Towne exploded. "They said so themselves after looking at him."

"Of course it wasn't. You weren't dumb enough to kill a blackmailer and throw his body in the river and hope to get away with it. You thought you were safe because Jack Barton was already buried in an unmarked grave in the Fort Bliss military cemetery."

Towne hunched lower in his chair. His face was livid, and his eyes were becoming mad. He leaned forward to tap an uneasy tattoo on the edge of the liquor cabinet. He said, "I don't know which one of us is crazy."

"You were," Shayne told him cheerfully, "to think you could get away with it. Though you almost did—

until I thought about comparing the fingerprints of the body from the river with those taken from Jimmie Delray when he enlisted under the name of James Brown. Then I realized that you had put the soldier's uniform on Jack Barton Tuesday afternoon and—"

Towne's hand darted inside the liquor cabinet. It came out clutching a sawed-off .38, a replica of the pistol taken from Carmela Telgucado in Juarez. Shayne dropped to the floor as Towne whirled on him, and a bullet whistled over his head. He had his own gun out, but a heavier report from the open window prevented him from using it.

Towne fell back with a .45 slug from a police revolver in his shoulder, and his weapon clattered to the floor.

Shayne nodded to the uniformed man leaning through the window covering Towne with a smoking .45, and said approvingly, "That was nice timing."

CHAPTER TWENTY-FOUR

Chief Dyer's face showed up disapprovingly beside the sergeant's. "What's going on in there?"

Shayne got up and strolled forward to pick up the .38 Towne had dropped. He told Dyer, "Why don't you come around by the front door, and we'll let Towne tell us all about it?"

Towne was crouched back against the wall, gripping his wounded shoulder with his left hand. He mouthed curses at Shayne while he kept an eye on the patrolman's revolver. Shayne turned his back on him and broke the sawed-off revolver. He dumped four snubnosed bullets out on the table and examined them. The soft lead of each bullet was notched in the shape of a cross like the two taken from Carmela's weapon.

He dribbled the four bullets into Dyer's hand when the police chief trotted into the library from the hallway. "There's the rest of your case against him. He killed Cochrane with a duplicate of his daughter's gun, after planting a recently fired empty in hers before he sent her across the border to lead Cochrane into the alley where he was waiting to kill him."

"That's another lie!" Towne shouted. "I was at home. Bayliss has already confessed using her pistol to kill Cochrane."

"Bayliss," said Shayne, "is in love with Carmela. Ballistics says only two of those exploded shells in her pistol were fired from it. That's another place you slipped up, Towne. You knew a comparison test couldn't be run on a dumdum *bullet,* but you forgot there are tests that prove which gun an exploded cartridge was fired from. You slipped an exploded shell from your gun into hers last evening—after you decided Cochrane had to die the same as Jack Barton died."

"I don't understand it," Dyer said peevishly. "Mr. and Mrs. Barton both said the body wasn't their son."

"That body wasn't." Shayne looked at the chief in surprise. "Haven't you been listening outside the window?"

"Ever since you opened it," Dyer growled. "I wasn't going to let that evidence against Carter and Holden out of my sight until I knew Towne had it safely."

"I figured you'd be close," Shayne admitted, "as soon as you put that tail on me. But I'm glad you stayed out of sight, because I wanted to push Towne into a corner where he'd feel like pulling his gun on me. I'd already figured he must have one just like his stepdaughter's, but I didn't know where he'd have it hidden."

Towne had stopped cursing. He sank into his chair, breathing hard. He reached for the *tequila* bottle and filled his glass to the brim.

Dyer watched him curiously, and then sighed, "I still don't get it about Barton and the dead soldier— nor Cochrane either."

"Cochrane was comparatively simple," Shayne told him. "A sudden decision without any previous planning. You see, Cochrane had finally figured out the secret of Towne's two silver mines. Remember that

Barton had hinted part of the truth to him, and the *Free Press* ran a story on the *Plata Azul* not long ago. Cochrane added them up the same way I did, and realized that Towne was just using his Big Bend mine as a blind to get Mexican silver from the *Plata Azul* into the country and smelt it as domestic silver. Then he checked into the *Plata Azul* and discovered it didn't even belong to Towne. He thought if Barton had gotten ten thousand, he could do as well or better. What he didn't realize was that Towne would kill a man rather than pay blackmail."

"What about Barton? I don't see—"

"Let's finish up Cochrane first," Shayne said. "He sent Cochrane away with a promise to pay off. Carmela had overheard Cochrane mention Lance Bayliss's name, and she insisted that her father tell her in what connection. So Towne began improvising. He spun a story about Lance being in Juarez, but warned Carmela he had paid Cochrane not to tell her, so when she phoned Cochrane his denial wouldn't upset things. She made a date for Cochrane to take her to Papa Tonto's, and Towne planted one empty cartridge under the hammer of her gun. He hid in the alley until they entered it, stuck his gun against Cochrane, and pulled the trigger. Carmela shot twice at him without recognizing him in the darkness. Is that right, Towne?"

Towne had drunk half the *tequila* in his glass. He said, "It seemed like a good idea."

"It was," Shayne approved, "for a makeshift plan of murder. Nothing like as foolproof or elaborate as your other plan."

"Barton?" Dyer guessed hopefully.

Shayne nodded. "And a young soldier whom Towne induced to enlist under an alias. Jimmie Delray had been working in the *Plata Azul*," he went on conversationally. "Did he suspect what was going on there, so it was really killing two birds with one stone when you used him in your murder plan?"

Towne drank some more *tequila*. He nodded absently. "That's where I got the whole idea. He wrote me he was quitting down there and was coming to El Paso to give himself up to the army. I recalled he looked a little like young Barton, same build and all, and I saw a way to get rid of them both." He spoke in a faintly regretful tone.

"He had already planned to kill Barton," Shayne explained to Dyer, "but he needed a positive way of getting rid of the body so it could never be identified. He fed Delray some hocus-pocus about catching spies, and got him to enlist under an alias. That was necessary, because he wanted Jack Barton to be buried in Delray's uniform and he couldn't afford to have it shipped home where his mother would immediately know it wasn't her son. It was safe enough as long as it was buried here. Delray had just enlisted and no one knew him. In Delray's uniform, with his identification tags, after being choked and hit on the head and run over, the body looked enough like the unknown recruit to get by."

"Wait a minute," Dyer protested nervously. "I still don't quite get the bodies straight. Who was the naked man in the river?"

"That was Jimmie Delray. The soldier. The one Josiah

Riley actually saw Towne murder by the river. He
stripped the uniform off him and put it on Jack Barton,
whom he must have had tied up at the time, keeping
him alive until dusk, when he planned to kill him just a
few minutes before he laid the body in the street and
drove his car over it."

"So he did all that," Dyer muttered, "by himself?"

"It was smart and damned near perfect," Shayne
said wryly. "He reported it at once as a traffic accident,
and expected it to be accepted as one. With Barton's
body safely buried in a soldier's grave, he knew the
crime could never be proved against him even if Barton
did disappear and he was suspected. With no *corpus
delicti,* he was safe."

"It might have worked if it hadn't been for the
autopsy," Dyer exclaimed.

"That's right." Towne's voice was thick with drink
and self-pity. "That's when things started to go to hell.
What made you suspicious?"

"A letter from Jimmie Delray to his mother—and
being acquainted with you ten years ago," Shayne told
him grimly. "It didn't make sense—you rushing to the
telephone like an ethical citizen and reporting an un-
witnessed traffic fatality. It was out of character—
particularly with you trying to win an election. If you
had accidentally run over a soldier, I knew damned well
you'd keep right on driving without reporting it."

"Why didn't he do that?" Dyer exploded.

"Because he realized there'd be a much closer investigation into the cause of death if the man was found
lying in the street later. By reporting it at once, his story

was immediately accepted and no one thought of even looking for another wound."

Dyer still looked slightly bemused, but he went over and tapped Towne sternly on the shoulder. "Come along with me if you're sober enough to stand up."

Towne shambled to his feet, his right arm hanging loosely at his side. His bleared gaze swept around the library and settled on the briefcase. "Gotta take thish," he muttered. "Paid ten thoushand for thish sho Carter won't get 'lected."

Shayne picked up the briefcase and gravely placed it in his groping left hand. "That's right. It's all paid for."

"Hell of a lot of good it'll do him," Dyer said. "This doesn't leave us any candidate for mayor. He could have saved himself ten thousand if he'd known you were on to him."

"That," said Shayne cheerfully, "is why I got the money before I started needling him about murder." He patted the bulky envelope in his coat pocket and followed the others out.